Erle Stanley Gardner and The Murder Room

>>> This title is part of The Murder Room, our series dedicated to making available out-of-print or hard-to-find titles by classic crime writers.

Crime fiction has always held up a mirror to society. The Victorians were fascinated by sensational murder and the emerging science of detection; now we are obsessed with the forensic detail of violent death. And no other genre has so captivated and enthralled readers.

Vast troves of classic crime writing have for a long time been unavailable to all but the most dedicated frequenters of second-hand bookshops. The advent of digital publishing means that we are now able to bring you the backlists of a huge range of titles by classic and contemporary crime writers, some of which have been out of print for decades.

From the genteel amateur private eyes of the Golden Age and the femmes fatales of pulp fiction, to the morally ambiguous hard-boiled detectives of mid twentieth-century America and their descendants who walk our twenty-first century streets, The Murder Room has it all. >>>

The Murder Room
Where Criminal Minds Meet

themurderroom.com

Erle Stanley Gardner (1889–1970)

Born in Malden, Massachusetts, Erle Stanley Gardner left school in 1909 and attended Valparaiso University School of Law in Indiana for just one month before he was suspended for focusing more on his hobby of boxing than his academic studies. Soon after, he settled in California, where he taught himself the law and passed the state bar exam in 1911. The practise of law never held much interest for him, however, apart from as it pertained to trial strategy, and in his spare time he began to write for the pulp magazines that gave Dashiell Hammett and Raymond Chandler their start. Not long after the publication of his first novel, *The Case of the Velvet Claws*, featuring Perry Mason, he gave up his legal practice to write full time. He had one daughter, Grace, with his first wife, Natalie, from whom he later separated. In 1968 Gardner married his long-term secretary, Agnes Jean Bethell, whom he professed to be the real 'Della Street', Perry Mason's sole (although unacknowledged) love interest. He was one of the most successful authors of all time and at the time of his death, in Temecula, California in 1970, is said to have had 135 million copies of his books in print in America alone.

By Erle Stanley Gardner
(titles below include only those published in the Murder Room)

Perry Mason series

The Case of the Sulky Girl (1933)
The Case of the Baited Hook (1940)
The Case of the Borrowed Brunette (1946)
The Case of the Lonely Heiress (1948)
The Case of the Negligent Nymph (1950)
The Case of the Moth-Eaten Mink (1952)
The Case of the Glamorous Ghost (1955)
The Case of the Terrified Typist (1956)
The Case of the Gilded Lily (1956)
The Case of the Lucky Loser (1957)
The Case of the Long-Legged Models (1958)
The Case of the Deadly Toy (1959)
The Case of the Singing Skirt (1959)
The Case of the Duplicate Daughter (1960)

The Case of the Blonde Bonanza (1962)

Cool and Lam series

The Bigger They Come (1939)
Turn on the Heat (1940)
Gold Comes in Bricks (1940)
Spill the Jackpot (1941)
Double or Quits (1941)
Owls Don't Blink (1942)
Bats Fly at Dusk (1942)
Cats Prowl at Night (1943)
Crows Can't Count (1946)
Fools Die on Friday (1947)
Bedrooms Have Windows (1949)
Some Women Won't Wait (1953)
Beware the Curves (1956)
You Can Die Laughing (1957)
Some Slips Don't Show (1957)
The Count of Nine (1958)
Pass the Gravy (1959)
Kept Women Can't Quit (1960)
Bachelors Get Lonely (1961)
Shills Can't Cash Chips (1961)
Try Anything Once (1962)
Fish or Cut Bait (1963)
Up For Grabs (1964)

Cut Thin to Win (1965)
Widows Wear Weeds (1966)
Traps Need Fresh Bait (1967)
All Grass Isn't Green (1970)

Doug Selby D.A. series

The D.A. Calls it Murder (1937)
The D.A. Holds a Candle (1938)
The D.A. Draws a Circle (1939)
The D.A. Goes to Trial (1940)
The D.A. Cooks a Goose (1942)
The D.A. Calls a Turn (1944)
The D.A. Takes a Chance
  (1946)
The D.A. Breaks an Egg
  (1949)

Terry Clane series

Murder Up My Sleeve (1937)
The Case of the Backward
  Mule (1946)

Gramp Wiggins series

The Case of the Turning Tide
  (1941)
The Case of the Smoking
  Chimney (1943)

Two Clues (two novellas) (1947)

The D.A. Cooks a Goose

Erle Stanley Gardner

An Orion book

Copyright © The Erle Stanley Gardner Trust 1942

This edition published by
The Orion Publishing Group Ltd
Orion House
5 Upper St Martin's Lane
London WC2H 9EA

An Hachette UK company
A CIP catalogue record for this book is available from the British Library

ISBN 978 1 4719 0940 5

www.orionbooks.co.uk

THE *D.A.*

COOKS A GOOSE

by Erle Stanley Gardner

A midnight hit-and-run accident on a lonely mountain road . . .

a tragic fatality . . .

discovery of the missing car . . .

and Doug Selby, District Attorney of Madison City, finds himself not only up against a most involved case but in the hottest spot of his career.

AN ABSORBING CAST OF CHARACTERS INCLUDES:

—our sly, suave old friend, A. B. Carr, who needs no introduction

—a police chief with the instincts of a rat

—a strange couple from New Orleans who should have been co-operative, but weren't

—a hermit rancher with an incongruous past and a questionable will

—a female hitch-hiker who seemed to have thumbed the wrong car

—and a too philanthropic gambler.

And, of course, genial sheriff Rex Brandon and irrepressible Sylvia Martin, star reporter for the *Clarion*—and the lovely Inez Stapleton, Madison City's only woman lawyer, who finds the going tough when she tries to be friend and foe of Doug Selby at one and the same time.

1

DOUG SELBY, STANDING AT THE WINDOW OF HIS OFFICE, looked down on the heat-wilted activity in the street below. It was November, and the dry, enervating heat which comes to Southern California on the wings of a desert wind hung over Madison City in a pall.

The winter rains were long overdue. Fields were baked brown; hillsides, seamed and fissured with heat cracks, lay parched in the sunlight. Overhead the blue vault of a cloudless sky held a sun which shriveled every last remaining drop of moisture out of the dried vegetation below.

In these days of east wind, the humidity gauge registered zero. Microscopic particles of desert dust were in the air, dust so fine that it penetrated everywhere, even between one's teeth. And because paper had lost its tensile strength, shoppers carried paper bags with greatest care. The slightest strain, and the bag would rip with such suddenness that it seemed to explode, spilling purchases to the sidewalk.

For weeks now the desert winds had blown intermittently, and the rains had held off. Men's nerves were worn raw.

The door leading to the corridor clicked open, and Rex Brandon, the tall cattleman sheriff, grizzled with more than half a century of life in the open, entered the room.

"Hello, Doug. Looking at something?"

"No, just the street, and feeling a little proud, thinking about how differently these men take misfortune from those in the big cities. These people stand to lose everything they have in the world, but they're carrying on. Occasionally you see them look up at the sky— that's all. In the big cities when there's a crash in the stock market, you'll find a wave of suicides. You don't have that in the country."

Brandon said, "These people live out in the open, and have the boon of hard work. You could strip them of every possession in the world, and they'd still have something the city man couldn't buy."

"Health?"

"Not that alone," the sheriff said. "It's the feelin' of being a useful part in nature's scheme of things. Shucks, son, you know what I mean."

4

Selby nodded.

Brandon came and stood beside him at the window. He took a cloth tobacco sack from his pocket, spilled tobacco into the trough of a brown cigarette paper so dry that the noise made by the falling grains of tobacco was magnified out of all ordinary proportion.

Selby walked over to his desk, took a pipe from the upper left-hand drawer, tamped tobacco in it. His match exploded as he drew it along the underside of the desk.

"Hot," the sheriff said.

Selby nodded.

In this dry air one was unconscious of perspiration. It evaporated as soon as it formed, leaving the body hot and dry as though parched with a fever.

"What's new?" Selby asked.

Brandon said, "We've found the car that was in that hit-and-run accident last night—the one that wrecked Mrs. Hunter's car and killed her baby."

Selby's face tightened. "Good work. We'll make an example of them."

The sheriff said, "I'm afraid it isn't going to be as simple as that."

"Why?"

"The people who own the car claim it was stolen, and they're probably right."

"Who are they?"

"Name of Terry B. Lossten from New Orleans. Mr. and Mrs., staying at the Garver Rooming House."

"Where was the car?"

"They parked it on Palm Avenue near Central Street. There's no limit on parking there."

"Have it locked?"

"The ignition was locked. Someone short-circuited around the lock."

"The accident took place about midnight, didn't it?"

"Eleven-forty," the sheriff said. "Up on the mountain grade that cuts through to the San Francisco highway. Something should be done about that road, Doug. I notice some of the maps show it as a connecting link between the San Francisco-Los Angeles and the Los Angeles-Phoenix highways. It's shown as an unpaved road, but people who aren't familiar with this country don't appreciate how steep and high these mountains are. Just lookin' at it on the map, it looks as though you could take twenty-five miles of dirt road and cut off about thirty-five or forty miles of total distance."

"Was Mrs. Hunter coming down from San Francisco?"

"No. Going to San Francisco. This other car was coming down the grade, and the driver had been riding the brakes instead of using the motor compression. Mrs.

Hunter got over just as far as she could—too far. The other car sideswiped her over the grade. Killed the baby and bruised her up pretty bad. A woman riding with her was hurt, but not very seriously.

"Perkins is holding the inquest at seven o'clock tonight. Mrs. Hunter couldn't get the license number, but the woman riding with her got a glimpse of it. She says it's an orange license with a funny-looking bird in the center. That's a Louisiana license with a pelican on it. We telephoned the highway police in both directions. Well, the car was right here in the city, parked within four blocks of the courthouse."

"I thought you said it was stolen."

"It was—and returned right to the same place."

"Damaged much?"

"Very little. Just the fenders. . . . Mrs. Hunter's had hard luck. Her husband died two months before the baby was born—steel worker. She's trying to get workmen's compensation, claims his death was really caused by an injury he'd received a while back."

"What about the Losstens?" Selby asked. "How can they prove they weren't driving the car?"

Brandon took a last drag at the cigarette, pinched it out, and dropped the stub in Selby's ash tray. "Tobacco gets so dry these hot days it burns up in nothin' flat," he complained. "The Losstens claim they went to bed about nine. Garver, who runs the rooming house, saw them come in. They *may* have gone out again, but apparently there's no reason why they should. She's Ezra Grolley's sister. Grolley had a slight stroke about a month ago. Mrs. Lossten and her husband drove here from New Orleans to visit him. He had another stroke yesterday afternoon. I've got to go out there now."

"To Grolley's?"

"Yes."

"What for?"

"He's in a pretty bad way," Brandon said. "Think he'll probably cash in his chips. The nurse could tell there was something on his mind. He kept trying to tell her something. Finally he managed to whisper something about keys. She asked if he wanted his place locked, and his face lit up. He whispered, 'Sheriff,' so she asked him if he wanted the sheriff to lock up, and there was no question but what that was it."

Selby chuckled. "As I remember Ezra Grolley's shack, there wouldn't be anything worth stealing. Hasn't he some rabbits and chickens out there?"

"Uh-huh. His next-door neighbor's taking care of them."

Selby's mind reverted to the hit-and-run case. "Why should anyone steal an out-of-state car that's parked in

Madison City, drive up that steep grade, come tearing back down, have an accident, and then park the car at the exact spot from which it had been taken?"

Brandon shook his head. "You've got me, son."

"How about fingerprints?"

"That's another thing that makes it look as though the Losstens might be telling the truth. Bob Terry went over the steering wheel, the brake handle, and the gear-shift lever. They'd all been wiped clean of fingerprints last thing when the car was parked. Someone went over them with an oiled rag."

"The Losstens would have done that, if they'd been driving the car—and had thought of it," Selby pointed out.

Brandon nodded.

"What kind of people are they?"

"He's a carpenter, about fifty-five, a mousy little chap who looks squelched. She's forty-eight and wears the pants in the family, a big woman who says what she means and means what she says. Well, I'll go out and lock up Grolley's place. You'll be at the inquest, Doug?"

"Yes. I want to—"

Selby's phone rang, and the sheriff waited for Selby to answer it.

Selby made an effort to get the east-wind lethargy out of his voice. "Yes," he said. "Selby speaking."

A woman's voice burst into rapid-fire speech. It seemed to Selby that the words raced through his ears so fast they outstripped his attention.

"I'm Alice Grolley. I was at the bus depot with my little girl, and some people said the sheriff wanted to talk with me. I was waiting for some people at the time, and I'd stepped to the door of the station to see if they were coming; and these people asked me if I was Alice Grolley and I said, 'Yes,' and they said the sheriff wanted to see me, and to step out to the car, please. There was a car parked at the curb, and I went out to it and they said to get in, and when I hesitated, they pushed me right in the car, and said the sheriff wanted me right away. I'd left my baby on the seat there in the bus depot, but something in the way they acted frightened me, so I didn't say anything about her at all. I was afraid they might hurt her, and—"

"Where are you now?" Selby interrupted.

The woman's voice went right on without paying the slightest attention to the inquiry. "I want protection for the baby. She's in danger. Please send officers down to guard her. She's on the bench near the magazine stand. My baggage is there. You can—" Her sudden, high-pitched scream shrilled in Selby's ears. A man's voice

THE D.A. COOKS A GOOSE

said, ". . . that telephone." The jarring impact which followed might have been the sound of a blow or of someone falling. The receiver at the other end of the line was slammed violently on the hook.

Selby jiggled the receiver hook until he heard the voice of the courthouse switchboard operator. "Try and trace that call," he ordered. "Hurry!"

"Yes, Mr. Selby. I'll call you back."

Selby hung up, said to Brandon, "A woman. She said she was waiting at the bus depot. Someone told her the sheriff wanted to see her, and made her get in a car. She's left her baby at the depot on a bench near the magazine stand, and thinks the child's in danger. She talked like a house afire. Never stopped to draw a breath all the time she was talking."

He pushed back his swivel chair, put on his hat, stood by the telephone, waiting.

Brandon said, "I heard her scream over the telephone. Don't get *too* worked up about it, Doug. We get quite a few of those calls in the course of a year—people who have a persecution complex and get a little goofy."

"I heard a man's voice," Selby said, "and something that sounded like a blow."

"Sometimes relatives don't want 'em put in an institution. They try to keep 'em away from telephones."

Selby's telephone rang, and the district attorney had the receiver to his ear almost with the first tinkle of the bell.

The switchboard operator said, "I'm sorry, Mr. Selby. It was a dial call. We can't do a thing with it."

Selby said, "Thanks," dropped the receiver into place, said to Brandon, "Let's go."

As the men walked rapidly down the courthouse corridor, Selby said, "She was talking so fast it was hard to follow her. I understood her to say *her* name was Grolley."

"Probably something that sounded like it," Brandon said, "and because we'd been talking about Grolley, you associated the names in your mind. Bet you even money we don't find anything at the stage depot."

"You're probably right, but we're going to look anyway."

They reached the place where the cars of county officials were kept parked. The sheriff had his car backed to the curb so it would be ready for a quick getaway. "Hop in, son," he invited, "and hang on."

It was a matter of some six blocks to the Greyhound Bus Depot. The sheriff made it in a matter of seconds.

The depot was well filled. A man was closeted in the telephone booth. A woman waited outside, her shoulders drooped with weariness, a heavy bag on the floor beside her. A three-year-old child was crying fit-fully. Half a dozen people were lined up at the soda fountain. A tired old man sat on a bench staring at a life from which the vivid colors of youth had faded to a drab pattern. Three women were waiting for a bus, their toil-worn hands clasped on their laps. Aside from the fact that one was some twenty pounds lighter than the other two, they might have been triplets. There was the same look of patience on all three faces, the patience of women who have learned to conserve their energies to cope with life rather than rail at its seeming injustices.

By the magazine stand, on the plain wooden bench which served as a seat for waiting passengers, a man was engrossed in a magazine of true detective stories. A few feet away a Gladstone bag had been placed on the floor. On the seat above it was a Boston bag and a bassinet.

Selby stooped, peered into the bassinet, looked up at Brandon and nodded.

Brandon tilted his sweat-stained sombrero. "I will be doggoned," he announced.

Selby moved over to the magazine stand. A very blonde young woman with wide, blue eyes said, "Good morning. Was there something you wished?"

"That baby over there." Selby indicated the bassinet

13

with a motion of his head. "How long has it been there?"

"Gosh, I don't know, Mister."

"Have you noticed it before?"

"Yes. Yes, I saw it there, maybe ten or fifteen minutes ago."

The man who was reading the detective story magazine exhaled a long breath, closed the magazine, looked at his watch, and started toward the door.

"Just a minute, buddy," the sheriff said.

"Huh, me?"

"Yeah. How long *you* been here?"

"Since that Los Angeles bus came in. Why?"

"Was that baby there when you came in?"

The man frowned. "No. I think a woman was there. Wait a minute— Yes, that's right. The baby was there —that is, the basket was." He went on, somewhat apologetically. "I got interested in this story and wanted to finish it before I went out to do my business here."

"You don't know when the woman left?"

"No."

Brandon raised his voice. "Just a minute, folks. Look this way, please."

People turned to look at the rawboned, grizzled sheriff. "I'm the sheriff. I'm tryin' to locate this baby's mother. Anyone know where she is?"

There was a silence while people looked at each other, then one or two came tiptoeing forward to crane their necks at the bassinet. For a moment no one spoke, then several people started to talk at once, but to each other and not to the sheriff.

One of the three women who might have been sisters —the heaviest one—unfolded her hands from her lap. She said, in a calm, unexcited voice, "I saw her."

"How long ago?" Brandon asked.

"Perhaps ten or fifteen minutes."

"Did you see her go out?"

"No, I saw her come in."

"Through what door did she come, from the door to the buses, or—"

"No, from the street door."

"Can you describe her?"

"She wasn't very old. I dunno. Maybe twenty-five. . . . Did you see her, Hazel?"

The thin woman shook her head. The other woman sat calmly silent.

The woman who had been doing the speaking went on. "She had on a light-colored tan jacket—a little darker than the color of flax linen—and a skirt to match. The blouse was a light pink. She was a nice-looking woman. I remember she was wearing light tan gloves."

"Blonde or brunette?"

"Blonde— Well— Yes, I'm quite sure she was blonde."

"What's your name?" Selby asked.

"I'm Mrs. Albert Purdy."

"How long have you been here?"

"A little over half an hour."

"You're waiting for a stage?"

"Going to Albuquerque. I— That's my stage coming in now."

One of the big shiny buses swung in from the main street. There was a restless stir among the passengers. A man in uniform opened a swinging door marked EXIT and called, "Bus to El Paso via—"

"Hold that bus for a few minutes," Brandon called.

The uniformed man recognized him, said, "Okay, Sheriff, but we can't hold her very long."

A woman in the middle forties with thin, nervous features said shrilly, "Well, I declare! I never heard such highhanded goings-on in my life!"

"Just a minute, ma'am," Brandon said. "I don't aim to interfere none. I just want to find out who saw the woman who left this baby."

Apparently Mrs. Purdy was the only one. She gave the sheriff an address where she could be reached in Albuquerque, and Brandon gave the man at the door instructions to let the bus go on its way. "Well, son," he said to Selby, "it looks as though we've got a baby on our hands."

"And a kidnaping case," Selby said.

Brandon said, "If we look around at the public telephones near here, we may find this woman slumped down in the bottom of the booth where she can't be seen through the door. . . . Reckon we'd better get Otto Larkin on the job. . . . Ma'am, would you mind —you, ma'am, at the magazine counter. That's right— would you mind telephoning Chief of Police Larkin to come down here right away? If he ain't in, better tell whoever's in charge the sheriff and the district attorney are here and they'd like to have police on the job right away."

Brandon said in a lower voice to Selby, "Larkin will get sore if we start doing things without him. It's inside the city limits, so it's his case. The *Blade* would love to run a story about how we are muscling in on Larkin's territory. . . . All right, you folks, please don't stand around. If you didn't see the woman, there's nothing you can do to help except go on about your business."

The baby continued to sleep tranquilly in the basket, a sticky thumb held near its mouth. A persistent fly seemed particularly interested in that thumb, and Selby, feeling futile, and a little foolish, kept waving the fly away.

Otto Larkin appeared within less than five minutes. In the early fifties, he was inclined to carry too much flesh, and, in this weather, perspired freely. The perspiration evaporated instantly but left an oily coating on his skin, reflecting the light in a dull sheen, and making it seem that his fat was melting and oozing through the pores. His business suit of tropical worsted was bulged and wrinkled, but the police cap on his head was resplendent with gold braid. Selby gave the police chief the high lights, then outlined Brandon's theory that the woman had been slugged while using a public telephone somewhere in the vicinity.

Larkin scorned the telephone in the booth, but used the one on the counter of the newsstand. He gave instructions to headquarters to have a search made of every telephone booth in the vicinity. His voice was loud enough to carry over the entire depot.

"Well," Selby said, "we've got a baby."

The police chief stared at the bassinet and said, "Huh!"

"I reckon Mrs. Brandon could take care of it for a little while," the sheriff suggested, "until we decide what we're going to do."

THE D.A. COOKS A GOOSE

"That," Selby announced, relief in his voice, "is an idea! Think you'd better telephone her?"

Sheriff Brandon's big hands scooped up the bassinet. "Nope. She'll be glad to do anything she can for the little shaver."

Selby picked up the baggage. "We'll be down at Brandon's house, Chief," he said to Larkin.

Larkin took some of the hot-weather sag out of his shoulders. "Okay, boys," he said as though accepting a responsibility which had proven too much for them, "I'll take charge here. Don't worry."

19

2

BRANDON'S FRONT PORCH WAS A COOL, VINE-COVERED retreat from the outer glare. A hint of moisture exuded from the green leaves and gave the sheriff and the district attorney a welcome respite from the dry heat.

Mrs. Brandon had shared her husband's life for some thirty years: cattle camps, dry ranching, and homesteading. She had never known great affluence, and had felt the bite of poverty only too frequently. She had seen hard-won assets dissolve into thin air; and her character had ripened in the process. She had learned to take life philosophically, and to attach importance only to the really important things. Things which were really worth while were the ones she could use, and her main creed of life was to be neighborly. She emanated an atmosphere of ability and stability, a woman who could cook for a thresher crew, lend a helping hand to a sick neighbor, or bring down a running coyote at two hundred yards with a single shot.

The child had wakened now, and Selby and Brandon, sitting smoking on the cool porch, could hear the fretful note in the baby's voice, a weary discomfort which registered a vain protest against a world that was proving itself tiresome and uncomfortable.

Brandon stepped to the door. "Can I help, Mother?"

Mrs. Brandon's voice drifted out from the kitchen. "I'm doin' all right. She'll quiet down soon as I get her bottle fixed."

"Ain't you got that fixed yet?"

"I've been bathing her. Poor little tyke. Travelin' on a bus without a bath. You get on back and talk to Doug. I'll take care of things here."

Brandon came back, grinning sheepishly. "Take off your coat and relax."

Selby slipped out of his coat, hung it on the back of the chair, put his feet up on the porch rail, and enjoyed the mellow fragrance of his tobacco.

After a while Mrs. Brandon came out to join them on the porch. She made no attempt to discount her years. Most of her life had been spent far from beauty shops, and the hard work she had been called on to do demanded muscles which couldn't have been developed on a diet designed to give women of fifty-five the figures of girls of twenty. As she occasionally expressed it, she ate hearty, slept like a log, worked like a horse, and enjoyed life. Something of that rugged philosophy had stamped itself upon her countenance so that observant strangers turned for a second glance when she passed them on the street.

Madison City had its society, a circle which Mrs. Brandon religiously avoided. But, on occasion, members of that circle, fifteen to twenty years younger than Mrs. Brandon, fighting vainly against a few extra pounds, had been heard to remark that they'd "let the whole diet go hang" if they could get the wholesome appearance of the sheriff's wife.

Selby always felt stimulated when he came under the influence of Mrs. Brandon, while she watched over him with a maternal solicitude coupled with a tact which made her careful to "keep her fingers out of Doug's business."

"What did you find out?" Brandon asked as his wife perched herself on the arm of a chair and let her competent housekeeper's eyes swing over the porch in a mental inventory of the things which needed to be done.

She said, "The mother's careful. I reckon she's been to a doctor to find out all about feedin' her child. There's a typewritten diet formula, feeding hours, and miscellaneous information in the handbag, together with clothes for the baby."

"How about the big bag?"

22

THE D.A. COOKS A GOOSE

"I haven't opened that yet. I thought perhaps you'd better be with me, Rex. Doug can sit here and smoke."

Brandon grinned maliciously at Selby. "The missus keeps you bachelors right outside of the fence when it comes to feminine secrets." He got to his feet, pinched out his cigarette with the care of a man who has lived much of his life in the saddle, and followed his wife into the living room. Ten minutes later he was back with a report.

"Get ready for a surprise, Doug."

"What?"

"She's Ezra Grolley's wife, and the baby is his four-months-old daughter, Ruth."

"Ezra Grolley!" Selby exclaimed.

"That's right."

"Why—why, I understood she was a good-looking woman."

"She is, too. There's a picture in the suitcase, a picture of her and Ezra, and you'd hardly know Ezra. He's all dolled up in a suit with a shirt and necktie."

"Where were they married?"

"San Francisco, about fourteen months ago."

Selby said, "I believe Ezra *was* away for a while. . . . I didn't know he had either the ambition or the money to marry. . . . At that, he's probably saved whatever he could get his hands on."

"Still got the first nickel he ever made," the sheriff agreed. "Let's go see him." He opened the screen door. "Take good care of the baby, Mother," he called.

Mrs. Brandon treated this remark as utter surplusage which did not warrant the dignity of a reply.

Brandon drove to the county hospital. The young nurse at the desk looked cool and capable. She told them Ezra Grolley had died half an hour earlier. He had lost consciousness shortly after he had conveyed to the nurse his wish that the sheriff lock up the cabin.

Brandon and Selby exchanged glances.

The nurse said, "I've notified Harry Perkins, the coroner and public administrator."

Selby said, "Let me use the phone, please." She handed it to him, and he called his office and then the sheriff's office. He said to the undersheriff, "Just checking up. Keep on the job. Have someone at the telephone all the time. That woman may call again and leave an address."

He called Larkin and learned that the officers had searched every telephone booth in the city without finding the slightest evidence. The chief of police was inclined to discount the entire situation. "Think you've got a baby on your hands," he said. "They don't leave 'em on doorsteps any more. They park 'em in bus depots and telephone the county officials." His chuckle showed he was enjoying the district attorney's discomfiture.

"You may have something there," Selby admitted. "Keep a man on the telephone, will you, Larkin, so that if a call comes in, you can rush right out?"

"Yep, we're doin' that," the police chief said, "but there won't be any more calls come in—now that you've got the baby. . . . What did you find out from the baggage? Anything?"

"Apparently the woman's Ezra Grolley's wife."

"Ezra Grolley!" Larkin exclaimed. "Didn't know he had a wife. What does Ezra have to say about it?"

"Nothing. He died half an hour ago. I'm telephoning from the hospital."

"Okay," Larkin promised breezily. "I'll sit on the wire."

"We're going out to Grolley's place and take a look around," Selby told him. "I've told the switchboard operator to put my calls through the sheriff's office, and Bob Terry is on the job up there, ready to dash out if he gets any call."

"Don't get steamed up about it," Larkin said easily. "I still think you've won a baby," and hung up.

Ezra Grolley's "ranch" consisted of ten acres, a few citrus trees, a vegetable garden, some chickens, and rabbit pens. A neighbor had been caring for the chickens and rabbits during Grolley's illness. His first knowledge of Grolley's death came with Brandon's announcement.

The sheriff correctly interrupted the look of dismay as the man tilted back a straw sombrero and scratched his head lugubriously.

"An administrator'll be taking charge," the sheriff said, "and the stuff'll be sold. He'll have the authority to pay for takin' care of it."

"That," the man admitted with relief in his voice, "is goin' to make a whale of a difference. There's quite a job here, particularly in this hot weather. . . . I locked that door padlock."

The sheriff unlocked the house. He and Selby went inside. It was hardly more than a shack, and while not dirty, seemed drab and smelly. Nails had been driven into the board walls, and Grolley's wardrobe hung on these nails; old leather coats, glazed with dirt, faded blue shirts, worn overalls. The shelf cupboard by the kitchen sink held a few dishes, some canned food, a loaf of stale bread. A woman would have at least draped a cloth over the shelves, but Grolley had seen no necessity for this finer touch.

A can of evaporated milk, two holes punched in the top, had collected a deposit of solidified yellow at the openings and a thin streamer down the side. The coffee pot was blackened tin. Frying pans of assorted sizes dangled from nails, their sides black with sooty incrustations. A tumbler which had once held jelly was filled with bacon grease. A sugar bowl, half filled with sugar, was gray with dust and crawling with ants. Cooking was done on a two-burner kerosene stove. A small bedroom contained an iron bedstead which had once been white. An old-fashioned dome-covered trunk was in one corner of the room. A big packing box had been converted into another receptacle by the simple expedient of putting hinges on the cover. Near the trunk was a cheap suitcase of pasteboard and imitation leather.

Sun, beating down on the single-construction building, made the interior like an oven. Brandon said, "Gosh, let's get some air in here," and slid back the windows. A car could be heard turning in at the rutted highway, and a moment later the tall, thin form of Harry Perkins came through the doorway. "What you got here, Rex?" he asked.

"Darned if I know," Brandon said with a grin. "I want to find out somethin' about his wife."

"His wife?"

"Uh-huh."

"I thought he was a confirmed old bachelor."

"Way I figured it," Brandon agreed.

"When you come right down to it, Grolley wasn't so old," Selby pointed out.

"No, I guess he was along in the fifties somewhere. Shucks, that makes him about my age," the coroner admitted, "but somehow I always thought of him as being old. . . . He always needed a shave. You never saw him in anything except overalls and jumper, with one of those light blue workshirts open at the neck. I understand the doctors told him he didn't have long to live after he had that heart spell this spring. What about his wife?"

"A woman telephoned," Selby said. "She said she was Alice Grolley. She'd left her baby in the bus depot. She said someone had told her the sheriff wanted to see her and had made her get in a car. She didn't have a chance to finish the telephone conversation. Someone jerked her away from the telephone and hung up. I heard a man's voice."

The coroner frowned. "How about the baby?" he asked.

"We went down and picked it up. There was baggage. It was Mrs. Grolley, all right, and there's a copy of a birth certificate and a marriage certificate.

"Apparently, when she packed up, she felt she might be put in some position where she'd have to prove who she was."

"That's the way it looks, all right," Brandon said.

"How did they force her in the car?" the coroner asked.

"We don't know. She didn't have a chance to finish talking."

"Well, let's see what we've got here," Perkins said.

Brandon tried the lid of the trunk. It was locked. He fitted one of the small keys on the key ring Grolley had given him, and clicked back the lock.

Brandon pulled up the lid. Perkins gave his characteristic dry chuckle. "My gosh, old Ezra *did* have a suit of clothes. There it is, all folded up. Say, what's the idea? He's got this trunk filled with canned goods."

"Then he ain't eating much except baking powder," the sheriff said, picking up one of the cans. He took off the top, looked at the interior, frowned, tilted it toward the light, then shook the contents out into his hand—a huge roll of ten-dollar bills.

"The damned old miser!" Perkins exclaimed.

"Told you he had the first nickel he ever earned," the sheriff said to Selby.

The coroner spread out the roll, thumbed through them. "Ten-dollar bills," he said. "Must be pretty close to a hundred of them here. A thousand dollars."

The second baking powder can yielded a roll of fifty

twenty-dollar bills. The next can produced two hundred five-dollar bills.

Working swiftly now in startled silence, the men went through the cans. There were twenty-two baking powder cans. Each can contained one thousand dollars in bills of various denominations.

The men looked at each other. It was Sheriff Brandon who broke the silence. "Don't that beat the Dutch! Here's a man with a fortune tucked away in his trunk, living as though he didn't have a dime in the world. About the only provisions he ever bought were stale bread and the cheapest bacon. I don't suppose he ever went to a movie, or subscribed to a magazine."

Selby pointed out the legal significance of their discovery. "This may make a sweet fight over the estate."

"We'd better make a careful search for a will right now," Brandon said.

"Understand his sister's here," Perkins commented. "She's mixed up in that hit-and-run case."

"Yes. The inquest set for seven o'clock tonight?" Selby asked.

"I postponed it," Perkins said. "That was one of the things I intended to tell you. I forgot all about it. Mrs. Hunter's strapped. She thought she could raise money if she got to San Francisco. I advanced her the bus fare. She'll be back tomorrow night."

Selby took a notebook from his pocket. "Friday night, seven o'clock?"

"That's right. . . . I understand the Losstens claim they were in bed when the accident happened."

"That's what they told me," Brandon said.

"Of course the witnesses just saw the car," Perkins observed thoughtfully, "not the person who was driving it. . . . Isn't there some law making the owner responsible, Doug?"

"Only in civil actions. In order to establish criminal responsibility, it's necessary to show actual operation of the car."

Quick steps sounded on the ramshackle porch. Knuckles tapped against the open door, and a girl's voice echoed merrily through the place. "What ho!" she cried. "A maid invades the bachelor's domain—a maid in search of news."

They heard her walk quickly across the kitchen. It was Sylvia Martin, star reporter of the *Clarion*. What the *Blade* wasn't, the *Clarion* was, in Madison City. And Doug Selby and Rex Brandon owed Sylvia a lot. From the doorway she looked at them suspiciously.

"What's the idea of all the mystery?" she demanded. "And what's the commotion about the abandoned baby in the bus depot?"

Brandon fished his sack of cigarette tobacco from the

31

upper left pocket of his sagging, unbuttoned vest. "You tell her, Doug."

Sylvia Martin turned laughing brown eyes to the young district attorney. "Kick through, Doug," she commanded. "I'm on the trail of a story."

"How did you get the tip to come here?" Selby asked.

"I've just been trailing you around."

"Then your coming here didn't have anything to do with Ezra Grolley?"

"No. Why? Is Ezra Grolley another story?"

Selby indicated the cans on the floor. "About twenty-two thousand dollars' worth of story."

Sylvia Martin whipped some folded newsprint from her pocket. "Give me the rest of it, Doug," she said, beginning to write.

Selby said, "He was married. Descriptions of his wife make her an attractive woman about twenty-seven or twenty-eight, and she's disappeared. A four-months-old baby girl abandoned in the Greyhound Bus Station is probably his daughter, and the sheriff's office is very much interested in the present whereabouts of the mother. You can dress it up with all the trimmings, but give it a spread. We want to locate that woman."

"Can you tell me how you got the tip to go after the baby, Doug?"

Selby thought for a moment, then said, "No. I think we'd better let that wait . . . as far as publication is concerned."

"What else is in the trunk?"

"That's something we're going to find out."

Brandon returned to the trunk. "Here's some papers."

The bundle was neatly folded, held in place with rubber bands, dry and brittle with age. Brandon said, "I reckon he ain't had occasion to look in these papers for quite some spell."

The rubber which had stuck to the outer papers broke as Brandon tried to pick it off. The pile of folded papers spread out in the sheriff's hand.

"There's a bank book," Perkins said.

"Two of them," Selby added.

They opened the bank books. They were from San Francisco banks. Each showed a savings deposit of twenty thousand dollars. The first was made in nineteen-thirteen. The second in nineteen-nineteen. Interest had been entered up to nineteen twenty-nine. There had been no withdrawals.

There was no will.

"Boy, oh, boy," Sylvia Martin whispered. "Will I go to town on this!"

3

ON FRIDAY MORNING THE "CLARION" CAME OUT WITH a great human-interest story. Ezra Grolley, widely known in Madison City as an eccentric bachelor farmer, who carried thrift almost to a point where it ceased to be a virtue, had died in a local hospital, leaving not only a comparatively large estate but a wife and baby. Up until nineteen twenty-nine Ezra Grolley had quite evidently been an alert businessman, making money with the rapidity with which money had been made in the era immediately preceding the big crash. Then something had happened. Grolley had come to Madison City, settled down on ten acres of land, had become a recluse and miser, until some sixteen months prior to his death when he had mysteriously vanished for four months. During that time he had quite evidently married, lived with his wife for several months, then returned to his farm, folded the suit of clothes in which he had been married into his shabby trunk, and resumed the even tenor of his miserly ways.

The wife and baby, journeying to his bedside to be with him at the last moment, had met with some misfortune. The wife had disappeared, leaving the child in the Pacific Greyhound Bus Station. It was possible that she had met with foul play or was the victim of amnesia. The authorities evidently had some information which they were not as yet divulging, but all persons were requested to notify the *Clarion* of any information concerning a young woman approximately twenty-seven years of age, slender, dressed in a light tan suit with a pink blouse.

By noon the sheriff had a report from officers in San Francisco, and he and Selby discussed that report over lunch. Alice Dollman, secretary to one of the executives in a local power company, had married Ezra Grolley on July twenty-third a year ago. The two had lived together until sometime in the latter part of October when there had been a separation, but apparently no divorce. Records showed that a child had been born on the nineteenth of the following July. A birth certificate was duly filed giving the name of the father as Ezra Grolley, and the child's name as Ruth. Ezra Grolley had evidently sent his wife money. She had, however, kept right on working. She had asked for a three-month layoff, had returned to work, and kept on with the daily grind until the preceding week, when she had suddenly resigned. Her employer knew very little about her private life.

When Doug Selby returned to the office, he found that he had a caller in the outer office. Doug looked at his visitor without enthusiasm. He had enough on his mind without having to cope with A. B. Carr. The notorious criminal lawyer had been a disturbing influence in the community ever since he arrived, bag and baggage, from the city and established a country residence in the exclusive Orange Heights district. Every time Doug had run into Carr it had meant trouble. A. B. Carr didn't belong in a tranquil rural community. There was every reason to dislike the man, yet Selby, against his will, found himself fascinated by Carr's poise, his mental agility, and calm assurance. Doug fully intended to say formally, "Good afternoon, Mr. Carr," but instead found himself stretching forth his right hand and saying, "Hello, Carr. What can I do for you?"

Carr shook hands and smiled, a smile which deepened the lines on his face, brought out the twinkle of the shrewd gray eyes. When he spoke, his voice was richly resonant. "Selby," he said, "I've reformed," and the smile deepened into a chuckle.

"Come in," Selby invited, leading the way into his private office.

In the big city, A. B. Carr was affectionately referred to by persons who needed a "mouthpiece" as "Old A.B.C." It cost money to retain Old A.B.C., but once he interested himself in a case, harassed district attorneys usually threw up their hands. The man had a keen sense of the dramatic, a chain-lightning mind of razor-blade sharpness. Give him twelve men in a jury box, and he could play on their emotions as an expert organist draws sound from the giant pipes of his instrument. If A.B.C. had gravitated toward the stage in his younger days, he would doubtless have been a great actor. As it was, he had amassed a comfortable fortune in his law business. He had several times tried to retire, but had found the excitement of the game too fascinating to permit relaxing his activities.

He settled himself in the chair across from Selby's desk, lit a cigar, and regarded the smoking end with thoughtful concentration. Selby knew this was a build-up, a carefully manufactured interest-arousing delay in stating his errand, but nevertheless he found his interest mounting. Certainly A. B. Carr would never have come to the office except upon a matter of major importance.

With the cigar glowing to his satisfaction, Carr

shifted his keen eyes to Selby, regarded the district attorney in shrewd appraisal, and said, "This time I'm interested in a civil case. I want to enlist your aid rather than drop monkey wrenches in the Madison County legal machinery."

Again the smile softened his features. Selby returned a slightly less cordial replica of that smile. "Go ahead," he invited.

But it was not like Carr to drive directly to the point until after he had properly prepared his audience. "The case," he said, "is interesting. There's not a great deal of money involved. The fee is negligible as far as I am concerned, but because it means so much to my client, I am anxious to bring the case to a satisfactory conclusion. Incidentally, Selby, it will mean a lot to me in the community."

"How so?" Selby asked.

"People here regard me as a big-city criminal lawyer. They look at me with curiosity, a certain awe, and some repugnance. I can fancy that when I walk down the main street of your city, the substantial citizens sniff the air for an odor of brimstone, looking down at my feet to see if I have cloven hoofs."

Selby laughed politely, but he was thinking rapidly. Carr wanted something, and it behooved Selby to be cautious.

"Therefore," Carr went on, "when I had an opportunity to take a case which would enable me to bring justice to an unfortunate working girl, I thought it might be a very good move."

"What," Selby asked bluntly, "is the case?"

Carr made a slight gesture with the hand which held the cigar, and remained for a brief moment silent and motionless. It was a pose which would have delighted a photographic artist who wished to portray strong masculine personalities in characteristic postures. The lawyer's face had etched into lines of strength. His pose held the assurance of power.

"I am representing Alice Grolley," Carr announced. "The widow of Ezra Grolley."

Despite himself, Selby showed surprise. He tamped tobacco into the bowl of his pipe. "What," he asked, "can I do for you?"

"I want you to find my client."

"I'm *trying* to find her," Selby said.

"May I ask just what attracted your attention to the case in the first place?" Carr asked.

Selby said abruptly, "I'm going to ask you a few questions first."

Carr's gesture was almost as though he were baring his breast. "Ask me anything you want," he said in a voice which radiated a frank desire to co-operate.

"How long have you been representing Mrs. Grolley?"

"About a week."

"Have you ever met her personally?"

"Yes."

"Where?"

"She came to my office."

"About a week ago?"

"That's right. That's the first time I met her."

"Your office in the city, or your residence here—"

"No, my office in the city."

"If it's a fair question, what did she want?"

"She understood that her husband intended to divorce her. She wanted me to arrange for a property settlement. In the event he didn't divorce her, she wanted to divorce him. There was a child about which she had never told the father. A most peculiar situation."

"You knew Ezra Grolley?"

"No. I gathered something of his character from what she told me."

"Could you tell me some of the high lights?"

"Grolley," Carr said, "was an interesting by-product of our modern civilization." He paused to take a couple of puffs at his cigar, then went on impressively. "He was a real estate broker, specializing in ranch properties. About nineteen hundred and twenty-four he entered the stock market. By nineteen twenty-nine he was worth something over three-quarters of a million dollars—on paper. When the stock market crashed, he lost money faster than he could total his losses. But he salvaged something from the wreckage.

"I wasn't able to get the entire story from my client, because I don't think my client got the entire story from her husband. Apparently that period of worry and anxiety caused a change in his character. Prior to that time, money had meant nothing in particular to him. He had thrown it away on occasion, and was always a liberal spender. A few hectic months gave him a horror of being without money. He couldn't spend a nickel without it hurting."

Old A.B.C. shifted his position. His resonant, courtroom voice gave magic to his words, seemed to bring the personality of the dead rancher into the very room.

Then he went on. "In June of last year he had some trouble which sent him to a doctor. The doctor suggested specialists in San Francisco. They told him that the terrific mental and nerve strain under which he had driven himself during those money-making years had wrought some permanent damage. They told him tactfully that the end might come rather suddenly, or that it might be deferred for some time. So Grolley decided to have one last fling, spend all of his money, and enjoy life. He returned to his old haunts, blew in some money on clothes, started spending. He met my client, and, strange as it may seem, fell in love—or else he was feeling terribly lonely. He was, of course, a much older man, but he was affluent, considerate, and sympathetic. My client became interested in him. They were married. For two or three months they lived a pretty gay life and were apparently happy. Then Grolley suddenly realized that, as between a life in the big city and his hermit-like existence in Madison City, he preferred the simple country life. The city environment no longer appealed to him. He'd lost his taste for night life and the noise and tempo of city life got on his nerves.

"He wasn't especially articulate. He tried to tell his wife something about how he felt the night before they separated. . . . He said that the information the doctors had given him had started him on a spending spree. He thought he was going to be happy. He wasn't happy. He couldn't live her life, and he knew that she couldn't live his. At the time, neither of them suspected there would be issue of the marriage. Even when she realized that she was pregnant she did not write him. She said he would have worried about it. He didn't want domestic responsibilities, and she wanted him to feel free to enjoy the last years, or months, of his life as he saw fit, without feeling that the results of his marriage would chain him to a form of life distasteful to him. She *never* told him he had a child."

"I take it you can prove all this?" Selby asked.

Carr raised his heavy eyebrows, waited for a dramatic second or two, and then said, "My dear man, I can prove every word of it, not by the testimony of my client, not alone by the records of the City and County of San Francisco, not by the testimony of mutual friends; but by the handwriting of Ezra Grolley—in letters, which, fortunately, my client turned over to me at the time of our first interview."

"Have you," Selby asked, "any idea as to what happened to Mrs. Grolley?"

Carr's mobile face changed expression. He became stern and solemn. "I am, of course, not in a position to make any statement on that. . . . By the way, I understand Grolley's married sister, Mrs. Terry Lossten, is here in Madison City."

"That's right."

Carr placed the tips of his fingers together, moved the cigar around in his mouth, puffing it slowly, thoughtfully. Then he removed the cigar to say very very slowly, giving his words peculiar significance, "Have you talked with her?"

"I haven't. The sheriff has. I expect to see them to-night."

"Tonight?"

"Yes. Their car was involved in a hit-and-run case."

Carr's eyes showed sudden keen interest. "Not the woman whose child was killed?"

"Yes."

"*Their* automobile?"

"That's right."

"Who was driving it?"

"No one knows."

"That inquest is tonight?"

"Yes, at seven o'clock."

"I think I'll be there."

Selby said, "All right, Carr, this conversation is confidential. Quit worrying about the law of slander and tell me what you know."

Carr started to speak, then checked himself. For a few seconds he smoked thoughtfully and in deliberate silence. Then he shook his head. "I *know* nothing. If I gave you my surmises, it might prejudice you—not against an individual, but in your interpretation of evidence. I prefer that you make your investigation uninfluenced by any preconceived notions."

Carr got to his feet at once, extended his right hand across the desk, and circled Selby's hand with long, sinewy fingers. "Selby, you and I are on opposite sides of the legal fence. I have, however, learned to respect your legal abilities and your integrity. Ezra Grolley's letters are in my possession. At any time you wish to examine them, you may do so. In those letters you will find that Ezra Grolley had no great affection for his sister. Good afternoon, Selby."

For a moment Selby contemplated spoiling Carr's dramatic exit by calling him back with a question, then he changed his mind. It takes a good actor to put dignity into half a dozen steps while his back is turned to his audience; but Carr managed it superbly.

4

SHORTLY BEFORE SEVEN O'CLOCK THAT NIGHT SELBY strolled into Harry Perkins' office. Just inside the door a woman with a livid bruise on her forehead, a bandaged cut on her cheek, and a leather brace on her left wrist stepped forward and asked, "Is this Mr. Selby, the district attorney?"

Selby bowed.

"I'm Mrs. Hunter."

Selby said, "I'm so sorry about what happened. I want to extend my sincere sympathies, Mrs. Hunter."

She blinked back tears, averted her eyes for a moment, and said, "Thank you, Mr. Selby," and then almost immediately demanded, "What have you found out about that woman who disappeared from the bus station yesterday?"

"Nothing yet."

"I read about it in the paper when I got back from

San Francisco. I made a hurried trip to raise some money. . . . She was in the bus station when I went in to catch my bus. . . . You know, Mr. Selby, I don't want to be presumptuous, but if you and the sheriff are keeping that baby, you'll need someone to look after it. It would be a job for me and if I could—"

"Wait a minute," Selby interrupted. "You saw this woman in the bus depot yesterday?"

"Yes. While I was waiting for the San Francisco bus."

"Could you describe her?"

"Why, I could tell more about the baby than about her. You know how it is when you've lost someone—a—" Her voice choked in sobs.

Selby, his eyes keen with interest, said, "I understand, Mrs. Hunter. You had just lost your own baby, and so you noticed this child more particularly than would otherwise have been the case. Is that it?"

She nodded. "I was thinking how fortunate that mother was to have *her* little girl with her. I suppose I was selfish, but I wondered why fate had to single *me* out, when there were so many other— No, I don't mean it that way either, Mr. Selby, but—"

"I understand," Selby interposed hastily. "This may be *very* important, Mrs. Hunter. Did this woman know you were interested in her baby?"

"Oh, yes. You see, she saw me staring, and . . .

Well, I guess I *was* a pretty tough-looking case. She seemed afraid of me, put her body between me and the baby, and that hurt me, so I explained that I'd just lost *my* little girl, and that's why I was interested in her baby. She was very sympathetic. She'd read about the hit-and-run case in the morning paper, and asked me a lot of questions. . . . I didn't want to talk about it."

"What did she ask you?" Selby asked.

"She asked me about the car, whether I'd seen it and in particular whether I'd seen the person who was driving the car and whether there was more than one person in it. . . . I didn't want to talk about it, but didn't want to seem rude because she'd been so nice. I kept trying to change the subject by asking her about her baby and how old it was."

"Did she give you her name?" Selby asked.

"Not *her* name, but she told me the baby's name— Ruth—and when she was born."

"Do you remember the date?"

"Yes. It was July nineteenth. I remember because my baby was born July fifth, and that would make her child just two weeks younger than Mary."

"Can you give me the exact time of this conversation?"

"Why, not the *exact* time, but I was waiting for the

San Francisco bus. It's due to leave at eleven-thirty-three. I think it was five or ten minutes late, perhaps around eleven-forty. . . . You could find out about that, I guess, at the bus depot."

"Where was she when you left?"

"Sitting right there. She said she was waiting for friends."

"Did she show you the baby?"

"Oh, yes. After I told her about Mary, she let me peek in at her baby. . . . And then I started to cry, of course, and she comforted me the best she could."

"I wonder if you can describe her."

"The woman?"

"Yes."

"She was perhaps four or five years younger than I. . . . I'm thirty-two. She had dark hair, brown eyes. She wore a light tan skirt and jacket, and a light rose silk blouse. There was a rhinestone clip at her throat. She had light brown gloves, and the baby was in a bassinet covered with a pink blanket that had white elephants on it. She said she was waiting for some friends. . . . She seemed rather nervous. She asked me if I knew anyone in Madison City, and asked me about Mr. Carr, the lawyer."

"What did you tell her?"

"I told her I'd heard Mr. Carr was a wonderful jury

lawyer. Then she said he was her lawyer. I gathered there was some trouble with her husband. I didn't want to pry into it."

"How long did you talk?"

"It must have been ten or fifteen minutes."

"And she seemed nervous?"

"Yes. I think she was."

"Frightened?"

"Not what you'd call frightened, but very nervous and— I don't know, Mr. Selby, but I've thought a lot about the interest she showed in the automobile accident. She kept coming back to that. Perhaps it was just curiosity. I don't know, but she asked me twice about the car that struck us and whether I'd seen it clearly. And once she asked if I thought the other car had *tried* to hit us."

The coroner entered the room. With him came the sheriff and members of a coroner's jury who had been examining the body of the dead baby. The little group carried with them something of the aura of death.

Selby said hastily, "I want to talk with you again, Mrs. Hunter, and I'd like to have you repeat your story to Sheriff Brandon. . . . This inquest will be just a brief formality. I hope you won't find it too much of a strain."

But the inquest was not just a brief formality. The coroner called Mrs. Hunter, who gave her story. He called Miss Margaret Faye, a twenty-two-year-old blonde with bovine blue eyes and a face which never changed expression. Under the coroner's questioning, it appeared she had suffered a slight concussion and nervous shock in the accident. She had been taken to a hospital and placed under the care of a physician, who had let her leave her bed only that afternoon. She would have to report to him each day for the next week and her physician had suggested she be allowed to give her testimony as briefly as possible. She had, she said, been employed as waitress in several restaurants throughout the country. She was hitchhiking, and Mrs. Hunter had picked her up, about twenty minutes prior to the accident. It was Miss Faye who had had the presence of mind to look for the number on the license plate of the automobile which was bearing down on them. She had seen it for a brief instant when it flashed in front of the headlights of the Hunter car, just before the crash. It was, she said, an orange license with a "boid" on it. She hadn't been able to get the number, but remembered seeing two sevens.

The coroner showed her the license plate taken from the Lossten automobile. The last two digits were sevens, and Miss Faye said that the license "looked like" the one she had seen. She pointed to the pelican and said that it was the "boid."

A. B. Carr, who had sauntered into the inquest room unnoticed, got to his feet, and in a rich, vibrant voice inquired, "May I make a suggestion to the coroner?"

Spectators swung about in their seats, craned necks, and Carr, standing at ease near the back of the room with his hand resting on the back of one of the benches, immediately went on without waiting for the coroner's permission. "I would suggest that the coroner take into consideration the possibility that this was not an accident, that Mrs. Hunter and her little girl were mistaken for someone else, namely, Alice Grolley and *her* little girl, that the driver of this automobile followed Mrs. Hunter out of Madison City, passed her on the grade, turned around, and drove back down at high speed with the deliberate intention of meeting the upcoming automobile at the most dangerous turn in the road and forcing it over the bank—the intention being to kill Mrs. Grolley and her baby."

And Carr bowed and sat down during that instant of motionless silence when the full effect of his verbal bombshell was crashing home to the consciousness of his listeners.

5

HAD CARR REMAINED STANDING, THE NATURAL RESULT
of his announcement would have been to make him the
target for questions. By resuming his seat as though his
contribution to the investigation had been completely
finished, he preserved the suspense of the moment, and
placed the initiative squarely in the hands of the coroner, who was at the moment hardly prepared to assume it.

Perkins looked at Selby, and Selby, interpreting his
unspoken request, said to Carr, "I take it, Mr. Carr,
you wouldn't make a statement of that sort unless you
had some evidence upon which to base it."

Carr sat for a moment motionless, just long enough
to emphasize the importance which was to attach to his
reply, then he said, "It was not a statement, merely a
suggestion."

Selby's manner unconsciously became that of an attorney cross-examining a witness. "Very well then, I take it you wouldn't have made such a *suggestion* to the coroner unless there had been some evidence which in your mind indicated the possibility mentioned."

Carr's manner was affably condescending. "My dear man," he said, getting to his feet and making a gesture that was a half bow with his head, a half sweep of his left hand, "I merely felt that it would be a good idea for the coroner to take that possibility into consideration."

"And you have no evidence to support it?"

Carr smiled. "None which I care to communicate." He sat down once more.

Selby said to the coroner, "Very well, if Mr. Carr has no evidence which he can communicate in support of such a contention, I see no reason for changing the course of the investigation."

Perkins said to Miss Faye, "Proceed with your statement, Miss Faye."

She seemed to need a moment to collect her thoughts, then went on, "Well, I can't tell you who was driving that car for the life of me. I saw the headlights coming down the road and knew the car was going to swing wide on that turn. I thought right away about getting the license number, and that was what I was looking for. I didn't see who was in the car. It might have been a man, or a woman, or perhaps two or three people. I don't know."

"But you saw the license?"

"I got a flash of the license. The headlights of that other car were right in my eyes, but there was just a second when the car swung around in front of *our* headlights that I had a chance to see the license, just in the blink of an eye.

"Right after that there was a crash, and the side of the car I was sitting on started sliding down, then the car rolled over. I guess I bailed out. I don't know just what did happen. I remember I was rolling along on the ground, and I saw the car roll over a couple of times on a steep, downhill slope.

"Mrs. Hunter fell out about the time the car rolled over the second time. The baby never did fall out. It stayed with the car."

"When did you lose consciousness?" the coroner asked.

"Not until after we were halfway to town. Then it was just a few minutes, I think, but it left me feeling all woozy. They took me to a doctor, and he put me to bed."

"But you are able to recall what happened after the accident?"

"Very well indeed."

"Please tell us about it."

"Well, after I was spilled out, I sat right there and saw that car roll and tumble for a couple of bumps, saw Mrs. Hunter spill out, and watched the car keep right on going—faster and faster. The car that had hit us had gone whizzing on down the grade, and there wasn't any other noise except Mrs. Hunter's screaming and the car rolling and crashing. It was awful. You'd hear it hit and roll, and hit again, and then glass would smash and other rocks would start rolling along, then there'd be another crash, and Mrs. Hunter would scream. . . . And after a while the car hit the bottom and quit rolling. For a little while there was the noise made by other rocks rolling on down, and then that noise faded away to just the trickle of little bits of gravel, and then there wasn't any more noise at all, except Mrs. Hunter's screaming, and she stopped for a minute, and things were calm and silent with the stars up above, all quiet-like.

"Then I got up and I found I could walk all right. There wasn't any light. Mrs. Hunter was moaning and crying, but we worked our way down the steep side of the canyon, stopping every little while to listen to see if we could hear the baby moving or crying. We thought she might have fallen out too. It was dark, and we slipped and slid around because we couldn't see anything at all, and we had to be sure we didn't miss the baby, or perhaps step on it where it was lying unconscious. . . . It was enough to give a body gray hairs."

"And you finally found the car?" Perkins asked.

"We finally got down to the car, without having heard anything of the baby." The witness paused for a moment, and then said simply, "And when we got to the car, we didn't hear anything either—because there wasn't anything to hear."

"Then what happened?" the coroner asked.

"We found the baby in the car. We had to grope around in order to find it. Mrs. Hunter was crying and screaming, and crooning to her baby and telling it that Mother was there, and nothing could hurt it, and then she'd scream, 'She's dead! She's dead!'

"It was dark as a pocket down there, and you had to feel your way around. I could smell gasoline, and I was afraid the whole thing was going to catch on fire. Water was running out of the radiator, and making gurgling noises, and the motor kept crackling like a motor does when it cools off fast. . . . Well, I finally got Mrs. Hunter started. She wouldn't let me carry the baby at all. I don't know how she *ever* managed to get back to the road. It was all I could do, crawling around and feeling the way. I went first, so as to find a way up through the rocks, and then up nearer the top of the canyon, we hit brush and had to break a way through that."

"How long before you got back to the road?" the coroner asked.

"It seemed like about a month," she said, so simply that there seemed nothing facetious or disrespectful in the answer.

"But it wasn't that long," the coroner prompted.

"No, of course it wasn't."

"How long was it?"

"Maybe half an hour, maybe longer. My wrist watch was smashed when I was thrown out. It stopped at twenty minutes to twelve. We had to wait a long time before a car came along. After a while we saw headlights, and a man picked us up, and took us in. While we were riding in, I got all woozy, and passed out for a while. When I got out of the car here at Madison City, I was still dizzy. A doctor put me to bed—and that's all I know."

"Thank you," the coroner said. "I think you've expressed it very clearly and very satisfactorily."

Once more Carr got to his feet. "If I might have the privilege of asking one or two questions," he said, "I think perhaps I could convince the coroner that it might be well to follow my suggestion. In view of the facts, I don't want to subject *this* witness to any further strain; but if the coroner will recall Mrs. Hunter to the stand, I can ask the questions of *her*."

Again the coroner looked at Selby.

Selby said, "I see no reason for permitting any such procedure. Mrs. Hunter has gone through an ordeal. She, too, is suffering great nerve strain. Before we permit her to be subjected to any further questioning, Mr. Carr should show some logical evidence supporting his theory. There is nothing in the evidence to indicate this was other than an accident. Certainly nothing to indicate that, up to the time he drove on after the accident, the driver of the other vehicle, whoever he may have been, was guilty of more than gross carelessness or intoxication. . . . Perhaps if Mr. Carr cares to elaborate—"

"Mr. Carr does not," Old A.B.C. interrupted in his resonant, courtroom voice.

Selby raised his own voice. "Then," he said, "I see no reason for subjecting Mrs. Hunter to such an examination. She has already testified. She has been through a very trying experience. The dramatic description of the accident which she has just heard has caused her to live over again a scene of great suffering. I see no reason for subjecting her to a further ordeal."

Selby nodded to the coroner and went on, "It is, of course, only my suggestion—only the way I see it."

"I look at it the same way," Harry Perkins said. "If Mr. Carr knows anything, he should tell me. If he doesn't, there's no reason to stir up a mare's-nest, asking questions about something that isn't in the evidence, and can't be brought into the case unless there *is* some evidence."

"Thank you," Carr said courteously. "It was merely a suggestion on my part. I will try to refrain from making any more."

A city police officer testified to locating a parked automobile registered in the name of Sadie G. Lossten. He had found it about eight o'clock Thursday morning parked on Palm Avenue just north of its intersection with Central Street. That was about two blocks from the Garver Rooming House. He identified the license plate as having been taken from that car. He noticed that the left front fender was badly crumpled, that the left front headlight was broken, that there were scars and scratches on the body of the car, and, on closer examination, that the ignition switch had been tampered with, that a wire had been so placed as to short-circuit out the ignition switch, that the witness had subsequently located Sadie G. Lossten in the Garver Rooming House.

The coroner called Sadie Lossten. She came marching forward, a woman in the late forties with broad, erect shoulders, big hips, generous arms and bust, a double chin, and hard, glittering, gray eyes. She insisted on assuming the attitude that Mrs. Hunter was personally persecuting her, and glowered at the mother of the dead baby as she delivered her answers to the coroner's questions. She and her husband had driven from New Orleans. Her brother, Ezra Grolley, was sick. She didn't know it at the time. They had intended to "stay with Ezra," had arrived about seven o'clock that night, had gone to Ezra's house, and found that no one was home. The house was open, the doors unlocked. Her husband had a flashlight. They had "looked inside" and then waited for nearly an hour. They were tired, and when Ezra didn't show up, they went to the Garver Rooming House. They had no money to squander on leaving the car in a garage, and put it on a side street, at a place where they had been told there was no parking limit. Her husband had locked the ignition switch. The doors were not locked. "It wouldn't have done no good to have locked them anyway," she explained. A piece had been broken out of the glass of the front left-hand door. Anyone could have reached in and opened the door from the inside. It wasn't a car that anyone would have wanted to steal anyway. She and her husband had had supper and gone to bed. They didn't get up the next morning until seven-thirty. They had breakfast, and about eight-thirty got ready to get the car to drive out to her brother's house. An officer was waiting for them in the rooming-house lobby.

The coroner asked her if she had known that her brother, Ezra Grolley, had married. Apparently the question disconcerted the witness. She shifted her eyes so that she was staring down at the floor and hesitated so long that the coroner said rather sharply, "Can't you answer that question?"

"I don't have to," she said. "It's none of your business. That wouldn't have anything to do with this case."

"Do I understand that the witness refuses to answer the question?"

"Right now I do. I'll think it over. Maybe I'll change my mind. It ain't anybody's business, and it hasn't got anything to do with this case. It looks to me like you're letting that man over there," and she pointed at old A.B.C., "put ideas in your head. Well, the way I look at it, if he wants to sit in the game, let him shove in his ante. What right's he got to draw cards when he ain't even in?"

Some of the jurors smiled broadly.

"When did you next see your automobile after you'd parked it Wednesday evening?" the coroner asked.

"When the officer took me down and showed it to me. . . . And I want that license plate back, too. We can't drive the car without a license plate."

"We're merely using it for evidence," the coroner snapped. "We let you keep it all day yesterday because you said you needed it."

"We certainly did," Mrs. Lossten said belligerently.

"And just to keep the records straight," Selby asked, "that license plate which was shown to the witnesses is the license plate from your automobile, isn't it?"

She studied Selby for a long instant before she answered the question. Then she said shortly, "Yes."

"Did your brother know that you were coming to visit him?"

"No. Anyhow not just *when* I was coming."

"You didn't write him to that effect?"

"No . . . not that I see that it's got anything to do with this hearing."

"Possibly it hasn't," Perkins admitted. "I was merely trying to get the record straight."

"How long," Selby asked, "were you in your brother's house the evening of your arrival?"

Her hard, glittering eyes became instantly hostile. "Say, who are you?"

Harry Perkins answered the question. "That's Mr. Selby, the district attorney. He frequently assists me in examining witnesses at inquests where there's the possibility of a crime having been committed."

"Well, no crime's been committed here."

"Negligent driving under certain circumstances may constitute a basis for manslaughter," Perkins pointed out.

"Well, I didn't do any negligent driving."

"But someone drove your car."

"You haven't proved that—not by a long ways."

"How long," Selby asked, "did you wait at your brother's house?"

"Oh, about an hour."

From the back of the room Carr asked in a voice which seemed to fill every inch of space in the room, "Ask her if she looked for a will while she was there."

Mrs. Lossten hitched herself forward in the chair. "You keep your mouth shut!" she shouted in a voice shrill with anger.

The coroner said, "Mr. Carr, the coroner cannot permit you to examine witnesses."

"I was merely making a suggestion to the district attorney," Carr said.

"And we don't care for your suggestions," Perkins added.

Carr got to his feet with dignity. "Pardon me," he

said. "I thought perhaps I might help clear the matter up."

"And I'd like to know in what capacity you're here," Perkins went on. "Whom do you represent?"

Carr smiled. "I am merely interested as a taxpayer and a citizen; and since my presence seems to be disrupting the orderly nature of the proceedings, I will withdraw."

And Carr made something of a ceremony of leaving the room.

Mrs. Lossten said to Selby, "I see now what you were driving at. All right, we were around there for an hour. *So what?*"

"Nothing," Selby said. "I merely wished to know. I have no further questions of this witness."

"That's all," the coroner said. "Mr. Lossten, you come forward and be a witness."

Terry B. Lossten was a mousy, mild-mannered man with a sandy mustache and a voice which was hardly loud enough to carry to the ears of the jury. He was obviously a few years older and some forty pounds lighter than his wife. After each question, his eyes shifted to Mrs. Lossten. Selby could not see that she gave him any signals, but she sat there with shoulders squared belligerently, staring at him with such intensity that it seemed as though she were trying to hypnotize him.

Lossten said they had driven from New Orleans to see his brother-in-law, that they had gone to Ezra's place, found it unlocked with no one home, that they were there "about an hour," that they decided Ezra had "had another spell" and "after about an hour" had got up and gone to a restaurant, then they had gone to the rooming house, and to bed. He was quite certain that neither he nor his wife had left the rooming house from the time they had turned in until the next morning when the police officer found them and asked them to come and look at their automobile.

Asked if he had ever heard his wife refer to a Mrs. Grolley or make any comments as to the amount of money she would receive in the event of her brother's death, Lossten said quickly that he "couldn't remember nothing about it." He went on to explain that Grolley was his wife's relative, that he didn't inquire into her affairs none, and she didn't have anything to say about his—which brought another broad smile to the faces of the jury.

The coroner looked at Selby, who shook his head. The coroner said, "That is all," and Lossten, leaving the witness stand, asked his wife in an audible whisper, "How did I do, dear?"

"Terrible," she said. "Shut up."

The coroner's jury fixed the responsibility for the death of the child on the shoulders of some person or persons unknown who had at the time been driving an automobile owned by one Sadie G. Lossten, and found further that the driving of the automobile had been in a criminally negligent or murderously willful manner —a finding which they would doubtless not have inserted in their verdict had it not been for the mystery which Old A.B.C. had managed to inject into the case, without giving the slightest tip as to what cards he held in his hand.

6

HARRY PERKINS MADE AN EXHAUSTIVE SEARCH FOR THE will on Saturday morning, and found none.

Two more bank books were found in an envelope fastened to the back of a calendar on the wall of Grolley's little shack. They showed checking accounts in San Francisco and Oakland banks amounting to some thirty-five thousand dollars.

Shortly before noon Saturday, Caroline E. Hunter filed suit against Sadie G. Lossten, alleging, on information and belief, that a car owned and operated by the defendant, Sadie G. Lossten, had been driven so negligently as to cause the death of the plaintiff's daughter, Mary Hunter, for which the plaintiff asked damages in an amount of fifty thousand dollars. A. B. Carr appeared as attorney for the plaintiff.

There was still no word from Mrs. Grolley. She had left her baby in the bus depot and disappeared without leaving so much as a single trace.

San Francisco police had managed to locate two fairly good snapshots of her by interviewing friends, and two more were revealed in a search of her apartment. These photographs were forwarded to Brandon, and by one-thirty Saturday, Brandon had posters ready for distribution. Metropolitan newspapers had taken an interest and published a photograph of the missing woman under the caption, "HEIRESS TO HALF MILLION MYSTERI-OUSLY DISAPPEARS."

The courthouse closed at noon on Saturdays, and Selby, looking forward to an afternoon during which he would be undisturbed, disconnected his telephone and settled down to clean up his desk, although he realized that the strange disappearance of Mrs. Grolley would keep returning to occupy his attention.

He filled his pipe, spread out a file of papers on which he was preparing a brief, and started working.

From the corner of his eye he caught little flashes of bright light dancing in a crazy pattern. He looked up with a start, and the light was gone. He returned to his book, only to see it again. As he looked up, it vanished, then suddenly appeared again, a bright spot jiggling back and forth in a wild dance.

Selby realized then what it was. He pushed back his chair and went to the window.

Standing on the sidewalk across the street was a tall,

neatly dressed girl intent on maneuvering the mirror of her compact to reflect the sunlight in intermittent flashes through the window of Selby's office. So engrossed was she in holding the little mirror at just the right angle, that for a moment she didn't see Selby standing at the open window, grinning down at her.

Selby raised the screen. "Hi, Inez. What is this, Boy Scout week?"

She laughed up at him as she snapped her compact shut. "Hello, Doug. What do you think of my S O S?"

"Handy little gadgets, those compacts."

"How about coming down and letting me in? You county officials get snooty and lock up your old courthouse at noon Saturdays."

"Right away," he promised. "Walk around to the front, and I'll meet you there."

Walking down the long corridor of the deserted courthouse, Selby realized that it had been months since he had seen anything of Inez Stapleton.

Before Selby had been elected district attorney, he and Inez had run around together quite a lot. As the daughter of Charles DeWitt Stapleton, owner of a controlling interest in the big sugar factory, Inez had been one of the town's most popular debutantes, and Doug Selby, a young, aggressive lawyer with his career before him, was one of the city's most eligible bachelors.

Then Sam Roper, the district attorney whom Selby had defeated, had given too much leeway to organized rackets and criminals. The county had demanded a cleanup. Rex Brandon, representing the ranchers and cattle interests, had tossed his sombrero in the ring for sheriff, and had persuaded Selby to make the campaign along with him as a candidate for the office of district attorney.

Thereafter, things had moved with swift rapidity. The new ticket had been swept into office. Selby found himself far too occupied to take time out for social pleasures. Then Inez Stapleton's brother, a typical rich man's son, got into trouble. Charles DeWitt Stapleton had trained the big guns of his political influence on Selby to keep him from prosecuting—and had underrated his man.

When the smoke had cleared away, the Stapletons, under a cloud, had moved away from Madison City. For a long time Doug lost track of Inez completely. Then one day she returned. She had studied law, passed the bar examinations, and was back in Madison City to stay, militantly determined to make a career for herself.

She had reconciled herself to the fact that the days when Selby could or would take time out for social pleasures were gone forever. Realizing that the young district attorney had acquired a new standard of values

---

and was, in the line of his duties, seeing more and more of Sylvia Martin and less and less of her, Inez Stapleton had adapted herself smoothly to the new order, seeking Selby out only when her practice brought her into professional contact with him.

"Hello, Doug," she said when he unlocked the front door to the courthouse. She looked up at him provocatively. "Wouldn't this be a swell day to be swimming in the surf?"

"Don't," he pleaded. "Lord, what I'd give to—"

"Isn't the District Attorney of Madison County at least entitled to Saturday afternoons and Sundays? . . . You stick around here, and they'll manage to keep you busy. You should get away over the weekends."

"Come on, let's go!"

Inez Stapleton grinned. "I can't. I'm working myself, but I just wanted to see if you could be tempted."

"You devil!"

"Doug, I want to talk to you—sort of business."

"All right. Come on up."

He escorted her up to his office, seated her, offered her a cigarette, and then filled his pipe.

"Doug," she said, as he glanced across at her through the blue haze of the first puffs of pipe smoke. "It's about A. B. Carr."

"What about him, Inez?"

"You like him, don't you?"

"I can't say that I like him. . . . There's something about him that appeals to me."

"A fascination, Doug?"

"Not exactly. He's clever. He's a consummate actor. He knows courtroom psychology. Everything the man does, every move he makes, is dramatic and impressive."

"You know how he's regarded among the better people here."

Selby said, "I'm not so certain that I do."

"People know he's crooked as a corkscrew. They don't want to have anything to do with him."

Selby puffed thoughtfully at his pipe. "People are sheep. When Carr first came to the county, there was a lot of prejudice against him. Of course, he almost slipped up on that Taleman murder case. It took all of his skill to extricate himself from that. . . . The man has no morals. He's made his fortune out of representing criminals, but he knows human nature, he's likeable, magnetic, has an agreeable personality, is a shrewd judge of character. . . . But, Inez, like it or not, he's gradually building up a circle of friends here."

"Including the district attorney of the county?"

Selby grinned. "I'll be frank with you. I distrust the man. I dislike everything that he stands for. . . . And he fascinates me . . . not the man himself, but his masterly technique."

"All right, Doug, that's what I wanted to warn you about."

"What?"

"Old A.B.C. is out to cook your political goose here in Madison County."

"Why do you say that, Inez?"

"Because I've heard comments here and there. I get around, you know. What worries me is the way you feel toward him."

"I'm not certain that you do know how I feel about Carr," Selby said, "because I'm not certain how I feel toward him myself. But don't worry. The man's not going to hypnotize me."

"He's done it already, Doug."

"What do you mean?"

"That inquest."

"What about it?"

"He managed to dominate the situation. He stole the show, tossed a monkey wrench in your legal machinery, and then walked out."

"He'd have done that in any event," Selby said. "A coroner's inquest isn't particularly dramatic. Carr is. Given an opportunity like that, Carr needs only to stand up and say something, and people strain their ears to listen."

"But you should have put him on the stand, Doug, and made him tell what he knew."

"I was afraid to," Selby admitted. "I think that was what he was angling for. He wanted a chance to talk."

"Well, he talked plenty."

"Not as much as he wanted to."

"He walked out."

"Yes, but he's too smart a man to talk where he can't control the attention of his audience and keep them breathlessly interested in what he's saying. If he'd had any information, he'd have been more apt to have given it to the coroner when he wasn't a witness. . . . No, I don't think he actually knew anything. He simply wanted to instill suspicion into people's minds."

"Well, he did that all right."

"That couldn't be helped."

Inez Stapleton said, "Mrs. Lossten came to me, Doug."

"You mean you're going to represent her as an attorney?"

"Yes."

"Claiming the estate?"

"That and defending a suit Mrs. Hunter filed against her shortly before noon today, a suit for fifty thousand dollars for damages for the death of Mrs. Hunter's baby."

"Is the automobile insured?" Selby asked.

"No. They haven't any money. They've barely been getting by. They couldn't afford to pay insurance."

"Where does Carr expect to collect the judgment in case he wins?"

"Out of the estate. See what he's doing, Doug? He's not only representing Mrs. Hunter, he's representing Mrs. Grolley too and—"

"You knew that he's representing Mrs. Grolley?" Doug asked.

"Yes. Mrs. Lossten told me."

"How did she know?"

"I don't know. She seems to be pretty well posted. She's told me a lot about Mrs. Grolley. The girl married Ezra purely and simply for his money."

"She had a child by him."

"I know. She married him for his money, and she thought having the child would bring them back together. She saw he was getting away from her."

Selby said, "Look here. Your client has only been in town since Wednesday. She couldn't have learned all of that during the short time she's been here."

"I think she's been doing a little investigating," Inez Stapleton conceded.

Selby said abruptly, "Inez, did you want me to do something?"

"It's going to put you in an awful spot, Doug, if you don't put that shyster, Carr, in his place and keep him there."

"He's not exactly a shyster. He's resourceful. He's quite probably unscrupulous, but, in his way, he's a genius."

"All right, we won't argue about it. I'm simply telling you that you've got to control him or you're finished politically."

"All right, Inez, you've warned me. . . . Now then, what is it you want? Something I can do for you?"

"Yes, Doug. I want you to locate the will."

"Ezra Grolley's will?"

"Yes."

"We've tried, Inez. Harry Perkins went out and looked again this morning. He—"

"Not there, stupid."

"Where?"

"Carr has it."

"Carr!" Selby exclaimed. "Why, your client had more chance to go through his things and—"

"Don't be naïve, Doug. The will was gone, of course, before Mrs. Lossten ever got to Ezra Grolley's cabin Wednesday. Carr wouldn't have taken Mrs. Grolley's case without making sure that there wasn't any unfavorable will lying around to cut the props out from under him."

"What makes you think Carr has it?"

"I'll tell you something. Carr was seen out near Ezra Grolley's cabin Thursday morning. A woman was riding in the car with him—a woman who wore a tan suit and a pink blouse. But there's no reason to believe that was Carr's *first* visit to Grolley's place."

"Where," Selby asked, "did you dig up that information? You can't have been representing Mrs. Lossten very long."

"No. She came to my office about an hour ago."

"And she must have given you this information."

"She did."

"She's been covering a lot of territory."

Inez Stapleton laughed. "She's the bark," she said, "but her husband's the bite. He's a shy-looking individual, but he certainly does get around. He's the brains of the combination; but you'd never know it to look at him. She's the one who reaches the decisions, but he's the one who gives her the facts on which to base those decisions. It's a peculiar combination."

"He impressed me as being rather a rabbit," Selby said.

"He isn't. He's a fox."

"And you think Carr has the will?"

"I'm almost certain of it, Doug. . . . I'm going to tell you something confidential. I have a letter that Ezra Grolley wrote to his sister less than thirty days before he died. He said that his heart was bothering him, and he'd been troubled with dizzy spells, that a doctor told him he had high blood pressure, that his arteries were in bad shape, and that he mustn't overdo or excite himself. He told her in this letter that in case anything happened to him, he'd made a will giving her his property. She hadn't heard from him for some time, then—"

"Have you any ideas about where Mrs. Grolley is?" Selby asked.

Inez snorted derisively. "One of these days you ought to get Chief Larkin to teach you a few of the facts of life. Mrs. Ezra Grolley is being kept under cover, and it's a damn good thing she is, too."

"Why?"

"Because Carr is afraid to have us take her deposition. There are some questions Carr doesn't want us to ask. I'm not at all certain, Doug, Ezra Grolley is really the father of her child. . . . Oh, it's slinging mud, but it's bound to come out sooner or later. . . . Well, anyway, Carr engineered that whole business. He wanted to make a build-up in preparation for a will contest, wanted to get sympathy for the child, wanted to get the baby put before the public as Ezra Grolley's baby. . . . And he *didn't* want to have Mrs. Grolley cross-examined. That was something he couldn't afford right now.

"So he worked it out all very cleverly. He had Mrs. Grolley leave her baggage, which very fortuitously contained the child's birth certificate and her marriage certificate, and he had her call *you* with a cock-and-bull story which simply couldn't be substantiated. It's absolutely absurd, Doug. I'm ashamed of you for falling for it. The idea of anyone forcing her to get in an automobile in broad daylight on the streets of Madison City!"

"You seem to know the hell of a lot about it," Selby said. "I didn't release any information about that telephone call."

"Well, I know about it. So what?"

"Who told you about it, if it's a fair question?" Doug asked. "Even the *Blade* didn't say who telephoned."

She laughed. "There's a leak. I'm not certain, Doug. I think it came from—" She stopped suddenly. "Well, anyway, there's a leak, and I was told about it. . . . It fitted in with what the *Blade* said, I was told."

"By whom?"

"By Mr. Lossten. He's quite a little sleuth. He mixes

around and keeps quiet, and somehow people talk to him."

"And you think Carr arranged the whole business?"

"I'm virtually certain of it, Doug. He wanted to introduce the baby to the people through the medium of the newspapers. And he picked you as sponsor. The baby is here. The woman was whisked off the scene. And not even the great Selby can cross-examine a four-months-old baby!"

"But look here, Inez. Until after Grolley died no one knew—well, it must have looked like rather small potatoes to a man who gets the fees Carr does."

"Don't kid yourself, Doug. There's going to be a lot more property involved even than you think. Ezra Grolley evidently was a very wealthy man. . . . And don't worry about Carr not getting his share. If you have the chance, ask Carr about Jackson C. Teel."

"Who's he?" Selby asked.

"He's a man who looks like an angel, and has a heart that's as black and hard as the top of a wood stove," Inez said bitterly. "He's the real party in interest. Ask Carr about him."

A sudden thought struck Selby. "Look here, Inez, have you considered the possibility that Mrs. Grolley never told her husband about the birth of the child?"

"I don't think she did."

"Then he died without knowing he was the father of a baby girl?"

"If he *was* the father."

"Then," Selby said, "no matter what he—"

Selby heard the sound of running feet in the corridor of the courthouse, then a pounding on the door of his office, and Brandon's voice calling, "Doug. Oh, Doug. Are you in there?"

Selby crossed the office and opened the door. Rex Brandon, pushing his way into the room, stopped suddenly at the sight of Inez Stapleton, then grinned, and removed his sombrero. "Hello, Inez."

"Hello, Sheriff."

The sheriff turned to Selby. "I don't like interrupting, Doug, but this is important. Think you could drop everything, and take a ride with me right now?"

Inez Stapleton got to her feet at once. "We're all finished, Sheriff."

Selby met the sheriff's eye. "What is it, Rex?"

"Something I think you'd better take a look at," Brandon said evasively.

Inez Stapleton smiled mockingly at Doug. "I'm on my way."

"We're going down," Brandon said. "We'll let you out."

The three of them walked down the long, echoing

corridor of the courthouse. Sheriff Brandon must have been impatient, for he kept a full step ahead of the other two. Occasionally he would lengthen the gap, then check himself and slow down, but he was always at least that one step ahead.

Brandon's car was waiting at the door of the courthouse with the motor running, but he said nothing of offering Inez Stapleton a lift, and Inez tactfully turned off at right angles to the direction in which the car was headed. " 'By, Doug. Think it over," she said.

"I will," Selby promised, and climbed in beside Brandon.

The sheriff rocketed the car into motion, sent it charging down the hill, his siren screaming for a right of way across the main street intersection.

"What is it?" Selby asked.

Brandon said, "We've found Mrs. Grolley's body. She was murdered."

7

IN THE LIGHT OF THE SHERIFF'S STATEMENT, IT TOOK Selby's mind a few minutes to rearrange the various factors of the situation so that they made any sense at all. While he was shifting the pieces around to his satisfaction, the sheriff's speedometer needle quivered over toward the right of the dial, his siren keeping up a steady, screaming demand for the right of way. The automobile flashed by intersections, shot through frozen traffic.

"Where is she?" Selby asked.

"You remember the Glencannon Ranch?"

"Why, yes. It's in litigation," Selby said.

"Uh-huh. The bank's trustee or receiver or something. The judge appointed them last Monday and told them to make an inventory of the property, including all the furnishings in the house."

"I understand that was done. They had their complete inventory on Wednesday noon."

"That's right," Brandon said. "Well, this afternoon the cashier thought he'd check up on it personally. He went down to the place, and found Mrs. Grolley's body in a bedroom. She'd put up a terrific fight. . . . Looks as though they took her there as soon as they got her in their car. She probably telephoned you from there. They caught her telephoning, dragged her away from the phone, and beat her to death."

"Why do you say 'they'?" Selby asked.

"Didn't she say 'they' over the phone?"

"Yes. I was wondering if there was any other evidence."

"I haven't been there," the sheriff said. "The bank cashier telephoned the office, and Bob Terry took the call. He dashed down to make sure it wasn't a false alarm. It wasn't. He telephoned me at my house, and I tried to call you at the courthouse. . . . Sounded like you'd disconnected your telephone, so I thought I'd probably find you up there working. . . . What did Inez want?"

Selby said, "She's representing Grolley's sister, Mrs. Lossten."

The sheriff said shortly, "Oh."

"And Old A. B. Carr filed suit for fifty thousand dollars against Mrs. Lossten on behalf of Mrs. Hunter."

"I suppose," the sheriff said, "he fixed *that* up there at the inquest."

"I don't think he did," Selby said. "I was talking with Mrs. Hunter before the inquest, and you'll remember she repeated her story for us afterwards. She didn't say anything about filing suit, but she had told me earlier in the evening that she understood Carr was a very fine lawyer, and when she saw Mrs. Grolley in the bus depot, Mrs. Grolley told her that Carr was *her* lawyer. After seeing Carr in action there at the inquest, it was only natural she should look him up sometime this morning."

"The Losstens haven't a dime."

"But if they could collect even a part of Grolley's estate, they'd have money."

Brandon shot through a boulevard stop onto the main highway. "Something to that," he admitted grimly. "The old fox! Representing Mrs. Grolley and the child *and* Mrs. Hunter. Heads I win, tails you win for old A.B.C."

The sheriff slid the car into a wide, screaming turn as a dirt driveway in between rows of well-kept orange trees opened up before them. He rode the brake hard as he sent the car into a skidding turn, and left a billowing cloud of dust behind them as he traveled for

some fifty yards to enter a yard in which stood a cater-
pillar tractor, a plow and a few farm implements.

At the north end of the yard was a barn, and a tank
house with an electric pumping plant. To the east, a
bungalow sat back in the cool shade of trees. Two auto-
mobiles were parked under a huge fig tree, and Brandon slid his car to a stop alongside the others, opened
the door, and jumped to the ground.

A choking cloud of dust which had been generated
by the speeding automobile drifted gently up to en-
velop them, and Selby was coughing by the time they
reached the front porch. The district attorney could
never quite accustom himself to the presence of death,
and there was a feeling of depression which gripped
him as he automatically stood to one side to let Sheriff
Brandon push open the door and enter first.

The living room was attractively furnished. Aside
from the layer of fine dust which had been swept in
by the desert winds, one might have thought the family
had merely left for the day, closing up the room to
keep out the heat. The same was true of the dining
room, but Brandon, hearing voices from a bedroom,
detoured through a bathroom and opened a door.

The assistant cashier of the bank was standing at a
window looking out. Bob Terry, who had recently been
promoted to undersheriff, was seated on the bed, his

knee held in his clasped hands. He was smoking a cigarette and talking.

"Where is she, Bob?" Brandon asked.

"In the next room," Terry said. "I've dusted around some for fingerprints. You want to go in now?"

Terry pointed his question by motioning significantly to the assistant cashier whose back was still toward them.

Brandon looked at Selby. Selby said, "Just a minute. Who discovered the body?"

The assistant cashier slowly turned, and Selby saw that his face still had a greenish hue. The man looked as though he were suffering from nausea which would shortly become acute. "I did," he mumbled.

"I know you," Selby said. "You're with the First National, aren't you?"

"Yes, Mr. Selby. I'm Elmer Stoker. I knew you before you became district attorney. Then I went to Berkeley. After I was graduated, I got a banking job in Oakland and was transferred back here about a month ago. . . . I'm Pete Stoker's boy."

Selby said, "Oh, yes, Elmer, I place you now. I knew I'd seen you before somewhere. I know your father quite well." He extended his hand.

Stoker shook hands. His finger tips were cold. Selby thought it might be the first time the young man had ever seen death. His face was a greenish ashen hue.

His lips were quivering, and Selby could feel the trembling of the man's hand as he shook hands. He was quite evidently suffering intensely, and as Selby looked at him, he said, "Mr. Terry told me I couldn't leave, but if I don't get out into the fresh air, I'll—I—"

Selby reached a quick decision. "All right, Stoker, I'll make it short. You came down here to check an inventory?"

"Yes, sir. I wanted to make certain everything was listed."

"You found the body in the bedroom?"

"Yes."

"Did you touch anything?"

"Just the doorknobs."

"How did you notify the sheriff's office?"

"The telephone hadn't been disconnected."

"Do you know anything else?"

"No, sir."

Selby glanced at Brandon, who nodded.

"Okay," Selby said. "Don't talk about details. You're going to be a witness. People will ask you lots of questions. Someone will ask you about something you didn't happen to notice. You won't want to make yourself seem ridiculous by saying you don't know, so you'll make a guess. Later on, when some lawyer for the defense gets you on the witness stand, he—"

"I understand," Stoker interrupted. "You can trust my discretion, Mr. Selby. . . . And I think it won't be necessary to— I—I've had just about all I can stand—"

"All right, go ahead." Brandon said.

Stoker, looking as though he might be violently ill within the next few seconds, walked rapidly across the room, down the corridor, and out the door.

"I figured that was the thing to do with him," Terry said, "but I didn't want to take the responsibility. She's in here."

He opened the door.

It was another bedroom, and bore the external evidences of a furious struggle. A mirror had been broken; bits of jagged glass lay on the surface of a dressing table and had spilled over to the floor. The mattress had been partially dragged from the bed. One chair was overturned, another splintered. Rugs had been balled up and slid into corners. A framed picture which had evidently been used first as a club, then as a missile, was a wreck in the corner of the room. Glass from this picture had slivered about the floor and mingled with the bits of the broken mirror.

The body of the woman lay sprawled face down. She wore a light tan suit. Selby could see the collar of a pink blouse, short dark hair, modishly cut.

Bob Terry spoke matter-of-factly. "Top of the head

caved in. Bleeding from nostrils and ears, not a great deal of blood. She must have been beaten up pretty badly. I noticed bruises on the legs and arms. There's a bad wound on the side of the cheek. Looks like a cut. I think it was a two-man job. One little man and one big man."

"How come?" Brandon asked.

"The little man," Terry said, "was just about her match. This stuff," and he swept his arm in an inclusive gesture, "wasn't done in a second or two. There was quite a fight going on here for some time. They were equally matched. Yet she died almost instantly, when someone struck her a terrific blow. The little man couldn't have done it. She was pretty evenly matched with him. Someone else came in, smashed her from behind."

Brandon said, "You're probably right at that. You notified Perkins?"

"Yes. He should be out here at any minute. He's bringing the medical examiner with him."

"Found any fingerprints?"

"A few here and there. I didn't want to touch the corpse or take her fingerprints until Perkins got here. Here's something else in the way of a clue—those bloodstains."

"What about 'em?" Brandon asked.

Terry said, "You can see just about what happened. She was given the first wound here. She ran across the room to that corner. You can see the drops of blood are spaced about every three feet. Over in that corner she received another wound, and ran over here by the door. Those drops of blood are about every eighteen inches. Then, by the door, she received that terrific smash on the back of her head, and she never moved after that."

"Then during quite a bit of the struggle, she must have been unwounded," Brandon said, surveying the wreckage of the bedroom.

"That's right. She fought for some little time before she got the first wound. I think she got the first cut by being hit with that picture. It looks as though it had been used for a club."

Selby, examining the blood spots, said, "What causes all these little irregularities around the sides of these spots, Terry?"

"It shows the height from which the blood fell. Blood is thick enough so that the drops have a tendency to explode into little fragments, depending on the height from which the drops fall."

"I notice these are all evenly patterned," Selby said. "The little spatters are uniform around the edges of the central blood spot."

"That's right. It's the height from which the blood falls which determines the amount of spatter on the edges."

Brandon, looking the room over, nodded slowly. "I'm inclined to agree with your two-men theory. How about it, Doug?"

"It sounds reasonable," Selby said, "or one of them *might* have been a woman."

Harry Perkins drove up with Dr. Trueman, the autopsy surgeon, and while the doctor was examining the body, Selby, feeling oppressed with the stuffy atmosphere of the house and the aura of death which permeated the closed room, walked out through the back door to stand under the shade trees in the rear. He was still there when a car roared up the drive into the yard and skidded to a stop. Sylvia Martin stepped out.

"Well," Selby said, *"you* get around."

"Don't I always read the *Clarion* for the latest news?"

"How did you get the tip?"

She laughed. "When the sheriff's car, with you in it, goes screaming through town, wide open, I don't call it a tip, I call it bank night. I climbed in my car and kept asking along the way whether you'd gone on past. When you hit the main highway, I was afraid you were on a through trip, but I tagged along for a ways, and then saw the skid marks where the sheriff had ground rubber off the tires swinging in here."

"You're getting good," Selby grinned.

"Aren't I? What's happened?"

"Mrs. Grolley's body."

"No, Doug! Honest to God?"

He nodded.

"Suicide?"

Selby shook his head. "If you saw her you wouldn't have to ask. A messy job, too."

"The poor little baby," Sylvia said. "That's an awful initiation into the world for her. . . . Now come clean! How did you get the tip to rush down there to the Greyhound Depot Thursday?"

"Mrs. Grolley telephoned. She said she was in danger, that she'd had to leave her child at the Greyhound, and asked me to get down there fast."

"Why didn't you kick through on that earlier, Doug?"

"I was afraid that if she were being held captive and the persons holding her knew to whom she'd telephoned, they might kill her."

"Evidently they knew," Sylvia said grimly.

"Well, it was an easy inference, judging from the fact that Sheriff Brandon and I went down after the baby, but I didn't want to confirm it—not in so many words."

As he was talking, he strolled away from the house over toward the tank house.

"Where are you going, Doug?"

"I thought I'd take a look for tracks to see if I could tell anything about what cars had driven in here."

"You can't, Doug. This dust is powdery, and the east wind has been blowing."

Selby pointed toward a leaky faucet in the side of the tank house. "It looks as though there's a patch of moisture under that faucet, and I think there are tracks running past the barn."

"It looks like it," she said, and walked with him out from under the cool shade tree, across the glare of the yard, to the tank house.

The dripping water had formed a little puddle which covered some four or five square feet. As they drew closer, they could hear the hissing noise made by the leaky faucet as it dripped water in a steady trickle. A car had swung around the barn, making a turn. Two of the wheels—apparently those on the left—had gone through the oozy patch of mud just as the driver had started to turn. It was possible to distinguish the marks of the front wheel from those of the rear.

Selby studied the pattern of the tracks. "A new tire

on that left front," he said. Suddenly he straightened, stared frowning at Sylvia Martin, yet seemed oblivious of her presence.

"What is it, Doug?" she asked.

"Of course," Selby said, "it isn't conclusive."

"What isn't, Doug?"

"That car," Selby said, "had a brand-new Skidless tire on the left front."

"How do you know?"

"You can see the Skidless pattern. It's distinctive. . . . I don't suppose you particularly noticed the Lossten automobile?"

"I noticed the crumpled fenders and the way the ignition switch had been tampered with."

"The two rear tires," Selby said, "were worn smooth. The one on the right front had traces of a tread, but the one on the left front was a brand-new Skidless cord."

8

SYLVIA MARTIN STARED DOWN AT THE IMPRINT OF THE automobile tires. "I don't see why that isn't conclusive, Doug," she said.

"It's evidence," he admitted, "but it isn't proof. Lots of cars have Skidless tires on left front wheels, and even if we could definitely establish that it was the Lossten automobile, we couldn't prove who was driving it. It would be the problem of that hit-and-run accident all over again."

"But the second time they pulled the alibi that someone else had taken their car without their knowledge, it would sound pretty thin."

"Each case has to stand on its own merits," Selby pointed out, "but the best way to handle this is to trap them into admitting they were in possession of their automobile at all times on Thursday after the officers released the car. To do that I'll have to find something to use as bait—something to make them want to convince us they had the car."

"How long on Thursday did the officers hold it?"

"I think until about ten-thirty. They found the car, as I remember it, shortly before nine. They had it photographed, had an expert mechanic look it over, and then returned it to Mrs. Lossten. . . . The coroner took one of the license plates just before the inquest, so he could introduce it in evidence; but he returned it to them right after the inquest Friday."

"Doug, you know almost the exact time this happened, don't you?"

"No. I know when I *think* it happened, but so far there's no definite proof. I'm hoping Dr. Trueman can fix the time of death within sufficiently narrow limits so we can really get somewhere. . . . You see, she telephoned me on Thursday just before noon. If she wasn't killed until late Thursday night, that means she was held prisoner for some time."

Sylvia thought matters over. "Yes," she said, "I can see difficulties. It might have been any car that had a Skidless tire on the left front. The track might have been made either one or two days before, or a day after, the murder, and even if it were the Lossten car, you'd have to prove who was driving it."

"That's it exactly," Selby said. "You can't convict a

car of murder. You have to convict the driver. . . . In other words, we're up against a case of circumstantial evidence. The defendant has the benefit of the doubt. If the evidence can be explained on any reasonable hypothesis other than that of guilt, the jury must take that explanation."

"Still, it seems to me you've got enough to arrest the Losstens on."

Selby shook his head. "I'm sitting tight."

"You're going to be sitting hot when *this* news breaks. 'District Attorney conceals news of vital telephone call from murdered woman.' The only way to smother that fire is to arrest someone and make some news yourself."

He laughed, and there was a certain grim mirthlessness about his laughter. "Go in that house," he said. "Take a look at the body sprawled on the floor, and you'll know how I feel."

Sylvia started for the house, then turned to come back to him. "Doug," she warned, "don't be *too* conservative."

"What do you mean?"

"Don't wait to get an ironclad case against them before you arrest them. If you *think* they're guilty, throw them in jail, and work up the details of your case afterwards."

His nod was a mere mechanical reaction of acquiescence. She realized that his mind was occupied with matters of proof, and that her words had hardly registered.

"Doug Selby, *listen* to me! I'm telling you something! You can't be *too* conservative. People are going to demand action. You're a public servant. You have to give the public what it wants. If you can get a reasonably good case against someone, make the arrest. People want action."

Selby pushed his hands down deep in his trousers pockets, stood staring down at the powdery dust which reflected the sunlight in a bright glare. "Action," he said thoughtfully, "is what people always shout for, yet it isn't what they pay me to get for them."

"What do they pay you to get?"

"Justice."

Sylvia Martin started to say something, then changed her mind, turned and walked toward the house. Selby moved over to stand in the shade of the fig tree. A piece of dry, straight-grained wood lay on the ground. He picked it up, took a sharp knife from his pocket, sat on the running board of the automobile, and thoughtfully whittled the piece of wood into a round, pointed skewer.

Fifteen minutes later, when Sheriff Brandon came out, Selby crossed over to him. "Rex," he said, "I suppose it's occurred to you that her baby may be in some danger."

Brandon nodded.

"I was going to suggest you drive by your house and break the news to Mrs. Brandon rather gently so as not to alarm her and—"

Rex Brandon interrupted him to say, "She'd never have forgiven me if I'd waited that long. I telephoned her ten minutes ago, Doug, told her what had happened."

"How did she take it?"

The sheriff said, "I've got an old forty-five I used to carry when I was riding line for the X-Bar outfit. The missus got so she could knock a tin can with it at fifty yards, nine times out of ten. . . . Well, Doug, that forty-five makes an awful big hole, and after what I told the missus over the telephone, she won't hesitate about pulling the trigger. . . . Sylvia tells me you've found some evidence out here in auto tracks."

Selby nodded.

Brandon said, "By the time we get a few more straws that point to the Losstens, we could tie them up into quite a bundle."

"That's what I'm afraid of," Selby remarked. "When a man's dealing with circumstantial evidence, he can't be too careful."

Brandon said solicitously, "Don't let Inez Stapleton influence you too much, son. You've been good friends quite a while, and I know you like her, but . . ."

Selby snapped his knife shut, dropped it in his pocket, and tossed the whittled stick of wood over toward the base of the tree. He said with sudden decision, "I'm taking a plane to San Francisco, Rex."

"Why, Doug, some clue?"

Selby shook his head. "We just don't know enough about this woman," he said.

Brandon studied him for a moment, then abruptly changed the subject. "Found her purse," he said. "She must have dropped it down behind the davenport."

"What was in it?"

"Some money, a driving license, some keys, fountain pen, social security number, compact, lipstick, handkerchief, and two rubber nipples sealed in cellophane, a card of safety pins, and a stub of a pencil which had been sharpened by someone who didn't know much about sharpening pencils, or who had a dull knife, or both."

"What does Dr. Trueman say about the time of death?"

"He can't be certain yet, but anyway not later than Thursday, and with you talking to her at noon he thinks it must have happened mighty soon after."

"Her purse was *behind* the davenport?"

"That's right."

"Could it have dropped there accidentally?"

"No."

"And if the murderers had wanted to conceal it, they'd have certainly picked another place to hide it."

"That's right."

"Then she must have dropped it there herself deliberately as a clue," Selby said.

"Clue to what?"

"She probably thought she was going to be taken somewhere from here, and dropped the purse as a clue. . . . Or else— Look here, Rex, there's no question as to her identity, is there?"

"Absolutely none. She has a wedding ring. There's a print of her right thumb on the driving license, and the photographs check."

Selby said, "Have Terry match her thumbprint with that one on the license, will you, Rex?"

Brandon said, "I did that first rattle out of the box. It checks. She's Alice Grolley all right."

Selby said, "All right, Rex, I'll try to get the five o'clock plane for San Francisco."

9

SELBY FOUND THE ATMOSPHERE IN SAN FRANCISCO WAS a sharp change from the desert-tanged, dry air of Madison City. Cold fog which had swept in from the ocean surrounded the street lights with a golden aura of suspended globules. The clanging bells of cable cars, the monotonous whine of mechanical fog signals and the deep booming of whistles from steamboats drifted upward through the fog mantle, muffled into a soft medley of sound by the thick white blanket which lay over the city.

The apartment house clung to the slopes of a steep hill. He pushed the button opposite the card marked *"Manager."*

The woman who answered the door was in the forties and fighting a courageous rear-guard action against advancing years. The toll of time showed only in those first almost intangible symptoms—rouge too generously applied, lip corners deliberately held upward by her cheek muscles so that her face gave the impression of having been frozen in a fixed smile. A certain heaviness of walk proclaimed the habitual use of a tight girdle.

She smiled at Selby with professional courtesy. "Did you want a single or a bachelor?"

"Neither," Selby said. "I'm the district attorney of Madison County. I'm interested in Mrs. Grolley and—"

"Oh, the woman who disappeared."

Selby said, "We found her this afternoon."

"You did?"

"Yes."

"Where?"

"In a house—dead."

The woman seemed unduly startled by this information. "The baby?" she asked.

"The baby's all right," Selby said.

"The police have gone through her apartment thoroughly."

"I want to do some more looking around."

The woman hesitated for a second or two, then said, "Very well, I'll let you have a passkey—but you'd better show me who you are first."

Selby produced credentials which satisfied the woman. She gave him a passkey, and said, "It's on the sixth floor, far back on the left. Apartment 619. Don't forget to return the passkey when you leave."

Selby rattled upward in a dimly lit elevator and walked down a thinly carpeted, poorly ventilated hallway flanked with inhospitable doors. He paused finally before the door on which the figures 619 were all but invisible in the reddish rays of a dim hall light. He fitted the key to the lock and opened the door.

The police had evidently made merely a routine visit. There was nothing to indicate an official tour of inspection save an open drawer in the bureau and the door of a clothes closet standing open.

It was a small apartment to have been occupied by a woman with a child. Scattered about the place were evidences of the child's occupancy. A rubber dog with a whistle imbedded in its underside so that it would give a shrill whistling bark when squeezed; a rattle, a teething ring, and a rubber pacifier were on the table. Also on the table were recent issues of several magazines, a book from a rental library, and an unopened package of cigarettes.

The pictures on the wall, Selby concluded, must have been part of the furnishings of the apartment. There were two exceptions. One was a framed photograph of Ezra Grolley, and Selby, who remembered the man only as an unkempt bachelor farmer, was surprised to see the familiar features peering out of the photograph from above a white collar and spotless cravat. The other picture was that of a baby girl, holding her big toe, grinning at the camera, and unconcernedly naked as the day she was born. It was obviously an enlargement from a Kodak picture which had been snapped right there in the apartment.

Quite evidently Mrs. Grolley had made up her mind to go to Madison City very suddenly.

Why?

Something must have happened to provoke such a sudden move. The logical reason, of course, was that she had received word her husband was seriously ill. That would probably have been in the form of a telegram, and, since the telegram had not been found in her purse, it was quite possible it was there somewhere in the apartment.

Selby started a detailed search.

In a pasteboard shoebox on a shelf in the closet, the district attorney found several stacks of letters. These letters had evidently gone unnoticed by the San Francisco police when they made an investigation at the request of Rex Brandon.

Selby settled down to read these letters, and, as he read them, became oblivious of the cheerless apartment in which closed windows had trapped stale, dead air.

He almost forgot that he was looking for evidence, for as he read letter after letter addressed to this woman who had been murdered, the full, dramatic story of her life began to unfold.

There were letters from Ezra Grolley, from Alice Grolley's mother, addressed at first to Miss Alice Dollman, then to Mrs. Ezra Grolley. The letters were invariably short, but pungent and to the point. The woman who signed herself simply "Mother" had an unsteady hand. She complained of her eyes, but her mind was clear and sharp, and she did not mince her words.

Of a clerk in whom her daughter had been interested, she had written, "If you think you can be happy with that drink of skim milk, it certainly is a love match. He doesn't have enough money to make it worth while. He couldn't have. Yet I can't imagine a girl marrying a scrawny-neck like that unless it's for love. However, don't let my ideas get you down."

Later on, a note of uncertainty crept into her correspondence. "These damn doctors have a system of ethics by which you pay them money to find out what's the matter with you, and all they do is satisfy their own curiosity. What they tell you is a formula consisting mainly of 'Don't worry.' . . . I don't know what to say about your Ezra Grolley. I've never seen the man. Your letters certainly sound enthusiastic. Knowing you as I do, darling, that's what worries me. You're too enthusiastic. Either you're trying to sell yourself on the idea, or trying to sell me."

That letter had been written some sixteen months ago. Six weeks later, Mrs. Dollman was under no illusion, either as to her own physical condition or as to the reason why her daughter was marrying Ezra Grolley. "Now you listen to me, Alice," she wrote. "I'm not as romantic about marriage as most hard-boiled women. I believe a first marriage should be for love. If that doesn't take, a woman is pretty apt to find her head makes a better guide than her heart—when she's doing it deliberately and for her own good. But you're not. You're doing it for me. My body has been doing a pretty good job for me a good many years, but the old mechanism is just about worn out. The doctors can tinker with it here, and tinker with it there, but, if you ask me, it's a hopeless job of cutting, a race between the scythe of Father Time and the surgeon's knife. I suppose this operation they want me to have will prolong life somewhat, and the ocean voyage would be a lot of fun to a woman who gets as much kick prying into the affairs of her fellow mortals as I do; but no operation is going to bring me back my lost youth, and every minute of an ocean trip would be a nightmare if I thought you'd purchased it by selling yourself on the marriage altar. I know you well enough to know that any advice I can give you won't make a great deal of difference, so I'm telling you here and now that if you marry, I won't ever take a cent of your money beyond the forty dollars a month you've been sending me. I'll keep on taking that, and that's every blessed red cent, even if you marry a man who has a first mortgage on the mint."

Three months later there was another letter, which said simply, "Oh, well, if you put it that way, I'll have the operation. I thought I could keep you from marrying, but, inasmuch as I couldn't and you've made the plunge and your husband seems to be such a generous individual, I may as well take what's offered. I'm sorry now I wrote you that I felt it was a marriage for money. You were too enthusiastic about him. I realize now how deeply you do care for him, and what a fine man he must be. After this operation, I'll come out and visit you."

But there were complications with the operation, and by the time she had recovered sufficiently to take the ocean voyage recommended by the doctors, she realized that her daughter had, after all, married a man she did not really love, and that the prospective arrival of a child was engrossing her daughter's attention to the exclusion of her husband.

Then came a series of postal cards: Havana, Cristobal, Barranquilla, Rio de Janeiro, Montevideo, and then a wireless from the captain of the ship advising Alice that her mother had passed away very suddenly.

There were letters from Ezra Grolley—reserved, businesslike letters although they dealt with the most intimate of domestic relationships. Selby found himself chuckling as his cold fingers held a sheet of paper dated at Madison City, addressed to Mrs. E. P. Grolley and reading, "My dear Alice: In reply to yours of the nineteenth, I am most interested and somewhat concerned to learn that there is a possibility of issue of our marriage. You will, I trust, keep me posted, and, in the event of developments as indicated in yours of the nineteenth, I will see that your allowance is increased by an amount amply sufficient to cover increased expenses incident to the event. Very truly yours, Ezra Grolley."

Selby laughed out loud, and then he frowned. Alice Grolley may not have advised her husband of the birth of the child. She may have appreciated his attitude toward family responsibilities sufficiently to have felt that the kindest thing she could have done would be to keep him from knowing he had acquired a social and domestic responsibility. It was only too evident that Ezra Grolley would not have regarded the arrival of a daughter as cause for particular joy or thanksgiving. But obviously he had been definitely advised of the possibility, and that in itself had legal significance.

After such a reaction from Grolley, it was possible that Alice had planned to wait a time, then go with the baby to her husband and see if the daughter couldn't awaken some fatherly interest. But the letter furnished unmistakable proof that Ezra Grolley had at least realized the possibility of issue from his marriage. This would certainly be sufficient to invalidate, as to the daughter, any will which might have been made and in which the daughter was not mentioned. A person who married after having made a will, was deemed to have revoked his will as to the legal share of the wife and child who might survive him. Or, on the other hand, had the testator made a subsequent will and neglected to provide for his child, without showing that such neglect was intentional, the will would be invalid as to the share which the child would take by law.

Old A.B.C. had told Selby that Grolley's letters to his wife had been placed in his hands by Mrs. Grolley. But why hadn't Mrs. Grolley taken these letters to give to her attorney?

Selby folded the letter, placed it in his pocket, and started reading through the other correspondence.

There were several letters dealing with financial matters, terse, business communications, then one which read:

"I think you have misinterpreted mine of the tenth concerning your allowance. I appreciate fully that you married me because you wanted financial aid for your mother. You made that quite plain to me at the time. I realize also the effort you made to make me a good wife. You succeeded. That it didn't work was due entirely to matters beyond your control. I have lived too much alone. Once milk has become sour, it can't be made sweet again. Having faithfully performed your share of the bargain, you are entitled to the benefits incident to the original consideration. Sincerely, E. P. Grolley."

Selby tied the letters in a bundle. These, he realized, were evidence, things which must be taken, labeled, introduced into court as exhibits, read to a jury. They were letters which gave him much of an insight into the character of the dead woman, told him something of Ezra Grolley's attitude toward her, but they gave no direct clue as to the identity of the murderers. Selby felt, however, that if Mrs. Lossten should produce any letter purporting to have been written by Ezra Grolley and stating that she was to be the sole beneficiary

113

under his will, that letter should be subjected to the closest scrutiny. He also wondered what letters Carr could possibly have that had a bearing on the marital relationship, since these letters he had discovered in Mrs. Grolley's apartment seemed to cover the situation completely.

Selby made another survey of the apartment, looking it over not so much for anything in particular as to get himself attuned to the personality of the dead woman, trying to soak up something of the environment in which she had lived, hoping that by so doing he might uncover something which would point somewhere.

It was in a drawer of the writing desk that he found several drafts of an unfinished letter that threw an entirely new slant on his problem. There was, however, nothing to show whether the letter had ever been finished and mailed.

There were three unfinished drafts. Each of the first two were filled with interlineations and cross outs. The first draft, once it had been revised to suit her, had been copied into the second draft. Then the second draft had been interlined and revised, and carefully copied on to the third sheet of paper. The fact that this third letter bore no revisions indicated that it might have been the final draft. This assumption, however, was contradicted by the fact that there was no salutation on the letter other than "Dear" followed by a blank, as though the writer had been uncertain as to just how to address the intended recipient, whether formally or informally.

The third draft said:—

"I presume you know by this time that E. has gone back to his home in Madison City—of *all* places.

"I know how deeply you care for him, and exactly how you feel about me. I am writing this so you will have my assurance that I have no intention or desire of trying to fan old flames into life. But it has become necessary for me to make a trip to Madison City. It's on an entirely different matter, something which I can't postpone any longer. I'm writing this so you won't misunderstand my reasons.

"At one time, I thought I really cared for E. It was just the foolish dream of a lonely woman who thought the differences in ages could be bridged.—I know better now, and I'm really glad he went back. He'll live his own life now—and I have my child. . . . Of course, I'll see him while I'm in Madison City. It would look strange if I didn't, but I want you to know that I am not going to encourage him. In fact, I think he realizes now how things stand. His letters are almost ridiculously stilted in their phraseology.—I'm so afraid you won't understand.—Even as I write this, I feel that you will completely misunderstand my motives and think I am going to Madison City to try and deprive you of something you feel will eventually be yours. I'm hoping you'll realize I wouldn't be writing you this letter if that were the case. After he first left, I could have simply crooked my finger, and he'd have come running back, even the baby wouldn't have—"

The letter ended there, and Selby, reading it with a furrowed brow, gave a long, low whistle.

It seemed incredible that Ezra Grolley could have been the apex of a love triangle. Selby could hardly conceive of one woman marrying him, let alone— Then, suddenly, he saw the matter in a different and more sinister light. What if this letter was not to some woman who was in love with Ezra Grolley, but written to Ezra's sister? Mrs. Lossten might have been in correspondence with Alice Grolley, and feared that Alice Grolley, young and attractive, could only too easily revive Ezra Grolley's affection, get the eccentric recluse to resume marital relations, and then at the time of his death step into the entire estate.

Selby wondered if Alice Grolley would have been so generous had she had any inkling as to the amount of money involved. . . . That letter was of the greatest importance as evidence. It indicated a motivation, a knowledge— And then, with the force of a sudden mental blow, Selby realized the legal problem with which he was confronted.

The letter was not evidence.

Even if he could prove that letter to be in the hand-writing of Alice Grolley, that it was intended to be sent to Sadie Lossten, he still could not prove that it had been sent, or that a fourth draft embodying the things which had been worked out in the third draft had ever been completed, let alone received by Sadie Lossten.

She, of course, would vehemently deny it.

Selby stood staring down at the letter. Several times before he had felt bitterly the manner in which the law tied his hands. Things which were plain, common sense couldn't be introduced in court as evidence because of foolish technical rules—arbitrary rules.

Of course, he realized that it would be unjust if Mrs. Lossten was to be bound by a letter which he couldn't show she had received, yet the circumstances under which he had found these documents indicated that Alice Grolley had not only written the letter, but sent it.

Her hesitancy over the manner in which she should address the recipient, the care which she had taken to express her ideas, all indicated that she was writing to the sister of her husband, a woman whom she had never met, whom she knew hated her. And Alice Grolley had been at a loss whether to address her as "Dear Mrs. Lossten," or "Dear Sadie."

Frantically Selby searched the apartment in the hope of finding some correspondence from Sadie Lossten which would show she had received this letter, some line of acknowledgment, perhaps some threat, something which would at least indicate that Mrs. Lossten had written giving her address, accusing Alice Grolley of having married Ezra Grolley for his money.

He found nothing.

Finally, when he realized there was no other correspondence to be found, he stood near the center of the room, hands pushed deep in his overcoat pockets, eyes staring with the fixity of his concentration.

He realized he was up against the problem which invariably confronts the conscientious district attorney. A piece of valuable evidence was in his hands. It was evidence which he could not legally introduce in a court of law. Was there, perhaps, some way to arrange the facts so that this evidence would become admissible?

While he was standing there, the various articles on the table indicative of the presence of a baby in the apartment arrested his attention. If he couldn't immediately work out some plan by which he could get his most valuable piece of evidence introduced in court, he could at least proceed with a routine investigation.

He switched out the lights, locked the door of the apartment behind him, but kept the passkey, and went to police headquarters where he introduced himself and said, "I want a fingerprint expert, someone who can develop some latent fingerprints and photograph them."

"How soon do you want him?" the sergeant asked.

"Right away."

"We'll see what we can do. Our best man is attached to the Homicide Squad. Then we have a couple—"

"This is a case which needs the best," Selby said. "A great deal may hinge on the fingerprint of a baby."

"Okay, come in and sit down. I'll see what I can do."

It was nearly three-quarters of an hour later that the sergeant introduced Selby to Clark Towner, a quick-moving, fast-speaking, nervous individual in the early thirties who listened to Selby's statement of what he wanted and said simply, "All right, let's go."

On the way to the apartment he explained he had been in a darkroom developing photographs of latents in a murder case when the sergeant had called.

Towner was completely engrossed in his profession, and talked shop to Selby all the time they were driving to the apartment where Alice Grolley had lived. Mostly his comments had to deal with murder cases, and, as he ran glibly from one to another, Selby found himself contrasting the isolated crimes which occurred in Madison City with the background of a city where police have not only to cope with the occasional crimes brought about by emotional instability, but with a professional criminal class which regularly makes its living through preying upon the rights of others.

He learned that in all big cities crimes were a regular part of the city life. Police could predict accurately how many homicides would be committed in a year, how many robberies in a month. It was information that showed sharp contrast to the peaceful life of a rural community, and Selby suddenly found something sinister in the fog-shrouded houses, parked cheek by jowl, leering at him from each side of the street—houses which imprisoned him to the narrow canyon of the city street. He was glad when they reached their destination.

Selby opened the door of the apartment with his passkey, switched on the light, and indicated the objects on the table. "I want the fingerprints of the baby who has been handling these," he said.

Towner tilted his hat to the back of his head, placed a small bag on the seat of a chair, opened it to disclose magnifying glasses, bottles, brushes, ink pads, papers, and films, his fingerprint camera, and some flashlight batteries. "We'll get 'em," he promised.

He started work at once, and while he worked kept up a running fire of conversation. "Things like these that a baby has handled are a cinch," he said. "Children's fingers are usually sticky—leave pretty good fingerprints."

Selby started prowling around the room again. In front of the dresser he stopped suddenly and frowned. There on the top of the dresser was a lacquered jewel case, and he felt absolutely convinced that it hadn't been there an hour before. He certainly would have examined it. Yet he realized there was a bare chance he might have overlooked it. He reached down and lifted the lid.

He saw an assortment of cheap costume jewelry, an antique brooch in the shape of a five-pointed star with a pearl at the apex of each point of the star. There was also an envelope addressed to Mrs. E. P. Grolley at the apartment address. The postmark on the envelope showed it had been mailed some two weeks earlier. The envelope had been opened by tearing it along the edge, as had been the case with the other envelopes in the pile of letters Selby had taken.

Selby shook out the folded letter. It was in the cramped style of Grolley's handwriting, and was couched in his usual stilted phraseology. It read, "Dear Alice: You may remember my having mentioned my sister. She is my only relative. In view of what the doctors have told me, I have naturally been thinking a lot about her and about our childhood together. I have written her at her last address and asked her to communicate with me. In the event she feels so inclined, I hope to persuade her to spend two or three weeks with me, not living in my house but upon some adjoining property which I can rent. That will enable me to get regular home-cooked meals.

"The doctor tells me that a part of my condition is due to eating irregularly, and improper food.

"In the event this matter turns out as I hope it may, the question of my intentions regarding my estate may arise. I have always felt closer to my sister than to anyone on earth and you will realize that it is only fair she should be properly provided for in the event anything should happen to me. A tie of blood which has lasted for a lifetime is more binding than that of a marriage which has gone on the rocks. The writer feels quite certain you will appreciate the matter in its true perspective and will fully appreciate her claims upon the writer's bounty.

"Trusting this finds you in good health, I remain, sincerely yours, E. P. Grolley."

Selby said to Towner, "How are you coming?"

"Coming fine. Have half a dozen good latents already."

"I'd like to have you take a look at this jewel case. Dust it off. See what you can find."

"Now?"

"Yes, please. It's rather important. I don't remember having seen it when I was here the first time."

"Think it's a plant?"

"I don't know. I simply want to make certain."

Towner dusted powder over the box, said, "Here's a fingerprint." He placed his glass over it, examined it, glanced sharply at Selby, shook his head, and continued to inspect the box. He dusted the inside, and then indicated the letter. "Want that, too?" he asked.

"Please."

Towner sprinkled it with a dark yellowish powder, then blew off the surplus particles. Selby saw some half dozen little smudges appear on the envelope. Towner studied them under a magnifying glass. "Same person," he said. "Here, let me take a look at your hands. I want the third finger of your left hand, the index and thumb of your right."

He examined the tips of Selby's fingers under the glass, said, "These are all your fingerprints."

"Any others?" Selby asked.

"None."

"Isn't that rather unusual?"

"*Very.*"

Selby went out to the kitchenette, found a string, tied it around the jewel case with the letters on the inside. Towner was now taking photographs, the camera pushed up against the rubber dog, taking a photographic likeness of one of the latent fingerprints to be developed.

"I can have these ready for you within two hours," he promised, "if you really need them."

Selby said, "I'm going to really need them."

10

IT WAS FOUR O'CLOCK WHEN SELBY REACHED MADISON
City, bringing with him prints of the latent fingerprints
of the baby which Towner had photographed, the jewel
case, and the letters.

There was still the feel of desert wind in the air.
It was cold now, a chill saturating the light, dry air.
Shortly after sunrise, this chill would vanish, giving
place all at once to the searing wind which dried out
crops and baked skins with an oven heat.

Selby slept until seven-thirty, then he took a shower,
shaved, and called Brandon, reporting briefly the things
he had discovered in San Francisco.

The sheriff said, "Glad you made that trip, Doug.
Had breakfast?"

"Not yet."

"How about coming out here?"

"No, thanks, Rex. I'll grab a bite uptown. I want to

go directly to the office. There are some things I want to investigate."

"Terry and I are having a conference in about half an hour. Suppose you drop in."

"I will," Selby promised.

He had breakfast in a downtown restaurant, drove to the courthouse, and found Terry and Sheriff Brandon in the sheriff's office.

"What's new?" Selby asked.

Brandon said, "Mrs. Hunter identified Mrs. Grolley's body as the woman she was talking to in the bus depot. There's no question about it."

"How about the baby?" Selby asked. "Has she looked at that?"

"Why, no," Brandon said. "We found the baby right where she told us. There can't be any— Say, wait a minute, son. Are you on the track of something?"

"I think I am," Selby said. "It may be more important to have the baby identified than we've heretofore supposed."

Sheriff Brandon gave a low whistle. "You mean that they might have beat us to it on the kid?"

"I don't know," Selby said, taking the photographs of the latent fingerprints from his pocket and passing them over to the undersheriff. "These are fingerprints of the Grolley baby. They were developed on some rubber toys, pacifiers and things. They look like dark smudges to me, but Towner, the San Francisco expert, said you wouldn't have any trouble checking them."

Terry looked them over, took a small magnifying glass from his pocket and studied the photographs carefully, then nodded reassuringly at Selby. "It'll be easy," he said.

"Well," Selby siad, "let's make an absolute identification. It may be important—if not in connection with the murder case, in connection with other things."

"Litigation over the estate?" Brandon asked.

Selby nodded.

Brandon raised his hand and scratched the hair along the back of his head. "Well now, son," he said, "don't you think it might be kinda bad for us to mix into that —even indirectly?"

"Why?"

"Well, there's Carr on one side of the fence, and Inez Stapleton on the other, with the probability that your murderer is somewhere in between. It's like the devil and the deep sea. If we get to foolin' around diggin' up evidence that either one of 'em can use to help get the estate, we're aidin' one or the other, and that's going to be bad. If we help out Carr's client, people will think he's so smart, he's slipped one over on us. If we help out Inez' client—the sister—people will say that's the one we should be prosecuting for murder. They'll say you've let Inez pull the wool over your eyes, and are using county funds to help her get proof so her client can reap the benefits of her murder."

"I know," Selby admitted. "There are two horns to my dilemma. If I don't get hooked on one, I will on the other. But I think it's my duty to get the evidence, regardless of whom it helps or hinders. . . . I found some letters that show what the real facts are—only we can never get the best piece of evidence before a jury—but I'm certain of one thing. The murder is tied up with the Grolley estate."

"You may be right at that," Brandon said.

"What's new on the murder, anything?" Selby asked.

Brandon said, "Well, here's everything we been able to uncover. Dr. Trueman fixes the time of death as being within a twenty-four-hour period ending not later than early Thursday afternoon. . . . That would make it seem they killed her very shortly after she called you on the telephone."

Selby nodded. "That's the way I've always figured it."

Brandon said, "Her purse was in behind the davenport with her driving license in it, also about a hundred dollars in cash. I already told you about that. She must have dropped it down there when they weren't looking.

. . . Now here's a funny one, Doug. Someone stole her gloves."

"Her gloves?"

"Uh-huh. She was wearing gloves when she went out to the house. She was even wearing gloves while that fight was goin' on in the bedroom. Someone took those gloves off after she was killed."

"How do you know she was wearing gloves?" Selby asked.

It was Bob Terry who answered the question. "Because there are no fingerprints of hers on any of the articles which she undoubtedly touched as she ran around the room trying to escape. There aren't even any of her fingerprints on the things she picked up to use as weapons. That means there's no question but what she was wearing gloves—and someone removed them after she was killed. And anyhow she'd have had her gloves. They're missing."

"What other fingerprints did you find?" Selby asked.

"None," Terry said. "—That is, none which can't be identified as having been left by the prior occupants of the house and the men who were taking that inventory for the bank. That means the murderers wore gloves, and *that* means premeditation."

"Mrs. Grolley's gloves weren't in her purse?"

"No."

"Why were her gloves removed after death?"

Sheriff Brandon said, "I figure it this way, Doug. There was no engagement ring, but there was a wedding ring with the initials 'E. G. to Alice' and the date 'July 23rd' engraved on the inside. I think the murderer wanted to keep the body from being identified as long as possible. That wedding ring was a very direct clue. After the woman was killed, the murderers wanted to remove the wedding ring. You know how it is in reaching for the left hand of a person who's facing you. . . . Nine times out of ten you'll grab the right hand instead of the left."

Selby nodded.

"Well," Brandon went on, "that's all there was to it. They pulled off the right glove first, then realized they had the wrong hand, pulled off the left glove, and probably the man stuffed the gloves in his pocket."

Selby fished his pipe from his pocket. "Then something happened to frighten them," he said.

"How do you get that?"

"If they took off the gloves to remove the wedding ring, and *didn't* remove the wedding ring, it stands to reason that something prevented them from doing it."

"That's right."

"Someone might have driven up to the house," Selby

said. "I wonder if Elmer Stoker didn't go out there sometime Thursday afternoon."

"We can damn soon find out," Terry said, and picked up the telephone to call Stoker's number. When he had Elmer Stoker on the line, he explained what he wanted.

Selby saw the undersheriff's face light with satisfaction. "Can you fix the *exact* time?" he asked, and then was silent for a few seconds, then said, "Elmer, that may be a highly important piece of evidence. Don't tell anyone about this. Go over the facts carefully in your mind to be certain there's no mistake. We'll get in touch with you later."

Terry hung up and said, "You certainly had a right hunch, Mr. Selby. We're going to be able to time that murder down to a split second."

"What did you find out?"

"Stoker was out there Thursday afternoon. He and a clerk named Sharpe went out to lunch together. They finished about twenty-five minutes after twelve. Elmer realized that he had thirty-five minutes on his hands before he was due back at the bank. He'd been thinking all morning, he said, that if he was going to be responsible for that property, he should do something about the pump. The pump was connected, and all a person had to do was to throw a switch, and it would run and overflow the tank, and might do some serious damage.

He suggested to Sharpe they ride out and check up on the pump. They rode out there and found there was an automatic shutoff device by which the pump shut off as soon as the tank was filled, and then cut in again when the tank was about two-thirds empty. That relieved his mind. He and Sharpe had to be back in the bank at one, so they jumped in the car, turned around and drove back fast."

"How long did they stay all together?"

"Not over two or three minutes."

"Did they notice any other car there?"

"No, but Stoker said that he noticed fresh tracks in the driveway. He didn't think anything of it at the time."

"He didn't know whether the tracks went both ways or only one."

"No, he didn't notice that. He assumed the car had gone in and out. He's probably been thinking it over. As soon as I asked him the question, he apparently knew what I wanted it for. He said he'd asked Sharpe about the tracks but Sharpe hadn't noticed them. By that testimony we can come pretty close to fixing the time of the murder."

"What time did they get back to the bank?" Selby asked.

"Five minutes before one. Let's figure that it would

take ten to twelve minutes for the trip. Now then, the murderers must have been in the house at twenty minutes to one. What's more, they must have just committed the murder, and were taking off her gloves when they heard Stoker's car turn in at the driveway. . . . You can imagine what a panic that threw them into."

Selby said, "That, of course, isn't positive proof."

"It may not be enough proof to convince a jury," Brandon said, "but it shows us just what time limit we need to cover. They murdered her very shortly after she telephoned you, Doug."

Selby said, "There's quite an interval at that. I got that call around eleven-forty. That must have been about an hour before Stoker drove up to the house."

"They may not have thought about taking her gloves off until a few minutes after the murder," Brandon said, "perhaps fifteen, twenty minutes, or half an hour."

"Well," Selby said, "those gloves may give us a good clue. . . . What does Mrs. Hunter say about them?"

"I forgot to ask her in detail," Brandon said. "She said that Mrs. Grolley was wearing this light brown suit and brown gloves. I think the other witness—the woman who was headed for Albuquerque—said the same thing, didn't she?"

"I think so. Let's concentrate on trying to locate those gloves. If Mrs. Grolley had them cleaned once or twice, we'll find a cleaner's mark in them. That will give us a means of showing they actually were hers. . . . If we find those gloves, we're quite apt to find the murderer along with them."

"And," Brandon said, "we'll start asking everyone where they were between eleven-forty and one o'clock on Thursday afternoon. That's going to help."

Sylvia Martin called Selby just as the district attorney was leaving the sheriff's office.

"Hello, Doug," she said. "Heard the latest?"

"What is it?"

"Treasure seekers have been digging around the Grolley property. I came out here to get some atmosphere for a human-interest slant and found the holes. . . . I found something else, too. I think you should see it just as I've found it."

"What is it, Sylvia?"

"I'd rather not tell you over the phone—something important."

Selby said, "Brandon and I will be right out."

He hung up the telephone, said to the sheriff, "Sylvia Martin's out at Grolley's place. She's found something."

Brandon reached for his sombrero. "All right, Bob,

you carry on. We probably won't be gone long. . . . Let's go in my car, Doug."

Sylvia Martin was waiting for them in front of the unpainted cabin, and the county officials stared at the holes which had appeared as by magic in the yard around the house. Some of those holes were three and four feet deep.

"They must have been digging all night," Sylvia Martin observed.

The sheriff frowned. "That's apt to make trouble. They didn't touch the shack, did they, Sylvia?"

She said ominously, "Come in here and take a look."

"But the door's locked."

"It *was* locked. It isn't now."

The hasp containing the padlock had been wrenched from the door. The door itself was ajar, and the interior of the cabin seemed dark and sinister as contrasted with the fresh morning sunlight.

"Watch your step when you go in," Sylvia cautioned.

The sheriff stepped across the raised threshold, then stopped abruptly with an exclamation of astonishment. The entire floor had been ripped up. The boards had been stacked on end in order to get them out of the way. There was an excavation in the bedroom directly under the place where the bed had been, a hole some three feet deep and eighteen inches in diameter scooped carefully out of the hard soil.

"Take a *good* look," Sylvia suggested.

Brandon dropped to his knees to peer down in the hole. "Shucks," he said, "looks as though they'd really found something here."

Selby, peering over his shoulder, saw the sheriff reach into the excavation and pull loose a piece of rotted sacking which had been packed around the sides of the hole.

"What is it?" Selby asked.

"Gunny sacking," the sheriff said. "This hole's lined with gunny sacks. Looks like they've been here for some time, too. The cloth's pretty well rotted. It's packed hard around the edges of the hole—kinda light-colored gunny sacks though—"

"Notice," Sylvia Martin said, "that there isn't any dirt inside the cabin."

"Meaning the hole wasn't dug last night?" Brandon asked.

"Partly that. . . . The hole must have been filled with something other than dirt."

Brandon said, "It looks as though someone had a tip and cashed in on it."

Selby appeared particularly crestfallen. "I should have thought of that, Rex. We should either have gone over this cabin with a fine-tooth comb or had a guard out here. How much do you suppose they found?"

"It ain't your fault," Brandon said. "It's mine. . . . And Harry Perkins has something to do with it. He was going to take charge and make a thorough search. . . . Gosh, there must have been a fortune in this hole, judging from the size of it."

"Perhaps," Selby said, "he kept his hard money here, either gold or silver."

"He may have at that," Brandon said, pulling out the half-rotted pieces of sacking. "This certainly is old stuff. It— Hello, what's this?"

Something white contrasted with the dark interior of the excavation. The sheriff reached down and took it out.

It was a bit of foolscap paper, folded into a long, narrow oblong. The outside was damp, and yellow discolorations had spotted the surface.

"Let's see what this is," Brandon said, taking his reading glasses from his pocket. He unfolded the document, glanced at it hastily, then handed it to Selby. "Give it a once over, Doug," he said. "It's a will."

Sylvia Martin said breathlessly, "Read it aloud, Doug."

Selby tilted the document so that the light struck the surface of the paper at a favorable angle. "It's all in his own handwriting," he said. "At least it purports to be. I've been seeing something of his handwriting lately, and it looks genuine. . . . It's in pen and ink. It's dated December fourteenth, nineteen hundred and thirty-five, and reads:—

" 'I, Ezra P. Grolley, being of sound and disposing mind and memory, having amassed a certain amount of property and having lived long enough to appreciate the futility of financial possessions, do hereby give, devise, and bequeath all of the property which I may have when I die to my beloved sister, Sadie G. Lossten, of New Orleans, Louisiana, the wife of Terry B. Lossten. In witness whereof I have signed my name this fourteenth day of December, nineteen hundred and thirty-five.' "

Selby folded the will. "Well, we were looking for it, weren't we?" he said wryly.

"It's signed?"

"Yes. Ezra P. Grolley."

"No witnesses?" Brandon asked.

"No. Witnesses aren't needed to a will which is entirely in the handwriting of the testator, if it's duly signed and dated."

"And I suppose," Sheriff Brandon said, looking down at the hole in the ground, "Sadie G. Lossten will claim we were negligent in caring for the property of the decedent, and as a result, a hundred thousand dollars was taken by persons who broke in."

"We're going to take an awful beating on this," Selby admitted, putting the will in his inside pocket. "And I guess we've got to hunt up Harry Perkins and break the news to him."

"A guard on the place?" Brandon asked.

Selby said gloomily, "No use locking the stable after the horse has been stolen, but we'd better have Bob Terry go over the place for fingerprints and try and find who did the digging and tore up the floor."

When Selby returned to his office he found a report from Bob Terry on the baby's fingerprints. There was no doubt about it. The prints he brought back from San Francisco checked with the prints of Mrs. Brandon's charge.

"So it *is* the Grolley baby," Selby muttered to himself.

11

MONDAY MORNING FOUND SELBY IN THE OFFICE OF SYD-
ney Bell Stone, a handwriting expert and examiner of
questioned documents.

Stone had the detached outlook of a scientist. He was
in the middle fifties with grizzled hair, a close-cut,
stubby mustache, and steady, gray eyes. He took the
documents Selby gave him, looked them over, and said,
"What do you want to know about them?"

"Are they genuine or forged?"

"You have some genuine signatures for standards of
comparison?"

"Yes."

"Let me see them."

Selby handed him several authenticated specimens of
the signature of Ezra P. Grolley, signatures taken from
such sources as he and Sylvia Martin had been able to
uncover the evening before.

140

Stone took them, glanced at them, and dropped them into a drawer.

"Aren't you going to compare them?" Selby asked.

"Yes."

"I mean now."

"No."

"Why?"

"It wouldn't do any good. I'm not the type of expert who glances at a signature, and then says it's a good resemblance or that it's a clumsy forgery, as the case may be, or that it 'looks like it's genuine.' In my opinion, all that stuff is worse than valueless. A man's opinion isn't worth anything unless it will stand up in front of a jury. A jury isn't interested in a man saying what he thinks unless they know what makes him think so. The only handwriting expert who's worth while is the one who reduces everything to scientific proof."

"You mean angles of stroke and all that?" Selby asked.

"That's a very small part of it."

"Could you begin work now—say on that will?"

"I suppose so. You can come into the laboratory if you'll keep quiet," Stone said.

"I can try," Selby told him, smiling.

"I'll do the talking," Stone said, as he led the way

into the laboratory. "You do the listening. Most people keep up a running fire of questions. I don't like it."

He spread the will on a glass table, switched on floodlights, and started to work. As he worked, he made terse comments by way of explanation: "These lights give daylight color values. . . . Take a look at the watermark on the paper. We put it over this ground glass with the powerful illumination underneath, switch on that light, and— There's the watermark—'Courthouse Bond.' Over there's a catalogue that tells when every brand of paper was first put on the market. . . . All right, we look up Courthouse Bond. If this will is dated nineteen thirty-five and Courthouse Bond didn't come on the market until a later date, we know right away the will's falsely dated. That usually means it's forged. . . . Let's take a look."

He opened the book, thumbed through a series of typewritten pages, then said, "No. Courthouse Bond has been on the market since nineteen hundred and twenty-two. Okay. That checks."

He closed the book, returned to the workbench, and said, "Now we'll take a look at the physical characteristics. . . . For instance, we first want to know about the ink. Most common ink is nutgall ink. Touch ink with a four per cent hydroxide of sodium solution, and it will turn dark red if it's nutgall, brown if it's logwood—"

The expert busied himself over the document and said, "It's nutgall. Now then, we'll test the color. We use a tintometer and register the exact color."

"Why the color?" Selby asked.

The expert glared at him over his microscope. "Nutgall ink changes color through oxidization. It takes about two years for it to assume its permanent color. In the meantime so that it will have a dark color, pleasing to the eye while the ink is oxidizing, the manufacturers put in a dye. There's a gradual cycle of change in color as the oxidization takes place."

"If this is over two years old then," Selby said, "as appears to be the case, the ink should have settled to its permanent color. Is that correct?"

Stone nodded and picked up various discs of colored glass, made numerical notations on the margin of a piece of paper. He studied those notations, then readjusted the light. Selby saw a frown come on his forehead.

"What is it?" Selby asked.

Stone said, "I'm not ready to tell you yet. . . . Let's take a look at that letter, the one where he says he's leaving all of his property to his sister."

Selby passed over the letter.

Stone examined it under the tintometer. Once more he made notations, then he turned around to face the district attorney. "I'm going to violate a custom," he said, "because I think the evidence is sufficiently conclusive."

"What," Selby asked, "have you found out?"

Stone said, "I want to put this will in a special oxidizing vault for twenty-four hours before I can give a final answer; but unless I'm very much mistaken the ink on that will is less than forty-eight hours old."

"Less than forty-eight hours!" Selby exclaimed. "Good Heavens, the physical appearance of the paper shows that—"

"I don't care a fig about that," Stone snapped. "There are literally dozens of ways of getting paper to assume those peculiar spots. . . . But I think you'll find this ink will change color very rapidly within the next twenty-four hours under the special concentrated oxidization treatment I shall give it. If that ink had been applied to the paper in nineteen hundred and thirty-five, it wouldn't change color at all."

"And the letter?" Selby asked.

"I'll let you know about the letter tomorrow."

Selby got to his feet. "Needless to say, this is highly confidential. I don't want anyone to know you have these documents or what your conclusions are."

"Naturally. Do you want me to telephone you?"

"Yes."

"I'll try and telephone you by two-thirty Tuesday afternoon."

Selby shook hands, drove back to Madison City, turning over in his mind the various ramifications of the situation. One thing crystallized into clarity. It was now his duty to subject Mrs. Lossten to rigid questioning.

Back in his office, Selby called Inez Stapleton, and, when he had her on the phone, said, "Inez, I want to talk with your clients, the Losstens."

"Doug, you and the sheriff are barking up the wrong tree. Why assume that just because she's Ezra Grolley's sister, she's guilty of all sorts of things? If you really want to uncover facts, go after Carr's client, and find out what he did with the will he stole."

"Carr's client?" Selby asked. "Which client? One of them is dead as a doornail. The other is Mrs. Hunter."

"Bosh and nonsense. Carr's client is really Jackson C. Teel."

"That's the second time you've mentioned Teel. Who is he and what's he got to do with the price of eggs?"

"If you really want the low-down, just tell Carr to bring his Mr. Teel to your office and see what happens."

"I'll think that over," Selby said. "In the meantime I want to talk with Mr. and Mrs. Lossten."

Inez Stapleton hesitated for a moment, then said,

"Well, Doug— You see— You're at your office now?"

"Yes."

"All right, I'm coming right over."

"Bring the Losstens with you."

"I'll be there right away, Doug."

But Inez Stapleton was alone when Selby's secretary ushered her into the office.

"Where are the Losstens?" Selby asked.

"Now wait a minute, Doug," she said. "I want to tell this in my own way."

Selby's eyes were ominously steady. "Go ahead," he invited. "Take your time and tell it straight."

Inez sat down in a chair across from Selby's desk, took off her gloves, spread them over her crossed knee. Her eyes avoided Doug's, and Selby noticed that her hands were trembling slightly.

"Well?" Selby asked.

She met his eyes then. She said, "Doug, you're making a fool of yourself on this case. You're being used as a cat's-paw, a tool. I told you not to get out on a limb playing around with A. B. Carr, and you've gone right ahead and got yourself out to where the leaves begin." The words came with a rush, as though having thought over this speech for some time and dreading the moment when she had to make it, she had, once that moment had come, rushed headlong into it in an attempt to get it over with as quickly as possible.

Selby said, "What does that have to do with my questioning your clients, Inez?"

"It has everything to do with it. There's a civil suit pending for damages. There's going to be a contest over Ezra Grolley's estate. Carr has very cleverly baited a hook, and you've grabbed it. I'm not going to let my clients be subjected to a lot of catechism, the purpose of which will be not to help you clear up the murder of Mrs. Grolley, but simply to give Carr a lot of ammunition which he can use in his civil suits."

"You mean you're not going to let me interrogate them?"

Inez Stapleton paused to swallow before she trusted her voice again. Then she said, "Doug, I'm—I'm awfully fond of you. I've known you for years. We used to be—well, pretty close friends. I admire you. But ever since you've had this job you've put your job and your duty before everything else in the world. You're probably right. But now I'll cite *my* job and *my* duty as the justification for doing what I'm going to do."

"What's that?"

Inez rose to her feet. "I'm going to keep my clients away from you until you come to your senses. I'm not going to let you be a stalking-horse for A. B. Carr, and if necessary I'll be quoted to that effect."

"I suppose you know what that means?" Selby asked.

"Of course I know what it means. It means that right now Carr is trying to find Mrs. Lossten to serve her with a subpoena so he can take her deposition in advance of trial. He wants to go on a fishing excursion just to see what he can pick up."

"Anything else?" Selby asked.

"Yes. You and Sheriff Brandon went out to Ezra Grolley's house. You took it on yourselves to lock it up and assume responsibility for it. You wouldn't turn the keys over to my client. She's the natural, the logical, and the legal person to take custody. She's Ezra Grolley's only living relative. She'd have taken charge of that place, and no one would have got in. But you and the sheriff took it on yourselves to keep her out.

"What happened?" she went on, her voice rising with indignation. "I'll tell you what happened. Persons who were able to think a little faster and a little farther ahead than the officials of this county went out and found a big fortune in bills buried under the bed—which was certainly a logical enough place to look. They went away with the money, and you'll never find out now who has it.

"And let me tell you something else, Doug Selby.

A. B. Carr is a slippery eel. He's twisting you right around his finger. He's crooked as a dog's hind leg, and you know it. He got out there to that cabin and stole Ezra Grolley's will. That's the first step in his campaign. The next one will be something you'll fall for like a ton of bricks."

"What's that?"

"He'll plant a forged will in favor of my client some place where you'll find it. You'll get all worked up over it, take it to a handwriting expert who'll pronounce it a forgery, and you'll immediately come to the conclusion it was forged by Sadie Lossten—just as Carr wants you to.

"No, Doug, until you see this thing in the right light, I'm going to keep my clients where you can't get information out of them that's going to help A. B. Carr."

Selby got up, walked over to the window, and stood staring out at the courthouse yard.

Inez got to her feet, walked quickly over to put a trembling hand on his arm. "Doug, can't you see it? Can't you please, *please* see it?"

Selby turned, picked up the phone, and told the switchboard operator, "I want A. B. Carr. Get him right away."

A moment later when Selby heard Carr's voice on the line, he said, "Selby talking, Carr. I want you to have your client at my office within an hour. Can you make it within that time?"

"My client?" Carr asked. "Do you mean Mrs. Hunter?"

"No. The one who's interested in the Grolley estate."

"Mrs. Grolley! Why, she's dead."

"I mean the one who's backing the show. The name is Jackson Teel."

There was a moment of silence.

"Well?" Selby asked.

"Very well," Carr announced, "we'll be there," and hung up.

Inez Stapleton's eyes were glistening. "Oh, Doug, I'm glad. . . . Did you know that Teel filed an application for guardianship of the person and estate of the Grolley baby late this morning? They produced Mrs. Grolley's will in Teel's favor and nominating him as guardian of her daughter in case anything should happen to her."

Selby's smile was grim. "If Jackson Teel knows anything, I'm going to find out what it is. I'm investigating this murder. I'm not going to leave any stone unturned."

"I know you won't, Doug."

"Now as far as you are concerned," Selby went on, "as you so aptly remarked, this is an official visit. You're an attorney representing your client, and I'm an attorney representing my client. It happens that my client is the people of this community. You either get your Mrs. Lossten here by five o'clock this afternoon, or I'll broadcast the fact that I'm looking for her, and that you're concealing her and refuse to produce her."

"Why—why—"

"You asked for it, and you're going to get it."

"But I tell you she's hiding, to keep Carr from taking her deposition."

"And I also want Terry Lossten," Selby said.

Her lips quivering with indignation, she said, "Doug, you're being very obstinate and—and foolish." She turned abruptly and left the office, chin up, shoulders squared—and Selby knew she was crying.

12

A. B. CARR USHERED JACKSON TEEL INTO SELBY'S OFFICE promptly at the appointed time. He performed the introductions with something of a flourish. Back of the courtly politeness of his manner, however, was a touch of the sardonic. It was as though he realized that Selby, having been tipped off to Teel's position, was on something of a fishing expedition, and Carr's manner indicated only too plainly that not only was his situation impregnable from a legal standpoint, but that Selby's investigations would be permitted to go only so far.

Jackson Teel was fat, a healthy fat which gave him a firm-fleshed appearance of joviality. Save for a hidden glint in the depths of the man's eyes, he seemed a typical specimen of a man who is enjoying good health, good fortune, and good food. Little radiating lines of humor were about his eyes. His lips smiled easily, and habitually. His graying hair, naturally wavy, rippled back from his forehead. His hand, freshly manicured, held a perfecto which filled the office with delicate aroma.

Carr said, "Well, here we are. My client has—"

Teel held up his hand. "That'll do, Carr. You're my lawyer. If I want to know anything about law, I'll ask you. Mr. Selby's the district attorney. He's sent for me because he wants to question me, and—" turning to Selby with a sweeping gesture, "—here I am, my boy, at your service. Anything you want to know I'll tell you. I have no secrets, none whatever."

Carr said cautiously, "There are certain private details of your business, Teel, which—"

"Which I'll communicate to Selby without a moment's hesitancy," Teel interpolated. "I'm familiar with Mr. Selby's reputation for integrity. I know he won't betray me. Anything I say to him will be in confidence. He's trying to clear up a murder mystery, and, by George, I'm trying to help him!"

And Teel nodded vigorously at his attorney and smiled happily at Selby.

Selby knew that this was a build-up, a carefully rehearsed scheme which had probably originated in Carr's fertile mind and which would give the interview its proper background, but he found himself smiling at the sheer artistry of it.

"What's your interest in this case?" he asked of Teel.

"What case?"

"The Grolley case."

"You don't mean the murder?"

"No, the estate."

Carr leaned forward and took the cigar from his mouth. Teel motioned him to silence. "Keep your shirt on, old boy," he said. "I'm going to tell Mr. Selby the whole situation. There's no reason why I shouldn't."

"On the other hand," Carr interposed hastily, "there's no reason why you should."

"Yes, there is, too," Teel contradicted. "Selby wouldn't have asked that question unless he thought it would help solve the murder mystery."

"But it has nothing to do with the murder," Carr pointed out.

Selby said quietly, "I'm very much impressed by the stage setting, gentlemen, but perhaps we can save time by getting down to business."

They looked at him then, and for a moment the twinkle left Teel's eyes, but it was back almost instantly and he said, "By Jove, you're right. Let's quit fooling around. . . . Do you ever play the horses, Selby?"

"No."

"Poker?"

"Occasionally."

"Do you like to win?"

"Doesn't everyone?"

"Well," Teel said, "I think it's something which is ingrained in human nature—in varying degrees. Now with me it's a passion, an obsession. I like to take risks, and I want to win. I hate to lose. When I lose I can smile all right, because I know that it's part of the game and because I know that I'm going to keep right on gambling and that the next gamble may be a win. If when I lost I thought I couldn't recoup my losses by doubling up on another bet, I'd be a pretty mean customer."

Carr said, "That's a poor thing to tell the district attorney."

"But it's the truth, and I'm here to tell the truth. I say, put all your cards on the table when someone calls your bet. . . . Well, let's get down to brass tacks. Selby, I like to gamble, and I like to win. I took a gamble on Mrs. Grolley. I wanted to win, so I protected myself against every contingency I could think of."

"What did you gamble?" Selby asked.

"I advanced her funds and agreed to stand back of her."

"In what?"

"In getting the right kind of a property settlement out of her husband."

"But her husband was willing to pay, wasn't he?"

"Not what I considered was reasonable."

"How much was that?"

Teel chuckled and said, "Well now, Mr. Selby, you're asking me something that I can only answer in one way. . . . There was just one figure I had in mind."

"What was that?"

"The biggest amount that I could squeeze out of old Ezra Grolley," Teel admitted with a disarming smile. "Yes, sir, Mr. Selby, that's the way I'm built. I squeeze a bargain for the last dime there is in it. When I win, I like to collect."

"You said you'd protected yourself?" Selby prompted.

"That's right. Before I put up any money, I always try to protect myself against anything which might happen. What bothered me most in this case was the possibility that while I was working on some settlement, Mrs. Grolley would fall in love. So I protected myself against that by having her agree she wouldn't proceed with a divorce action until I gave it my okay. . . . Of course she didn't know what I had in mind, but you can't marry someone while you're still married to another person." And Teel's fat diaphragm rippled with the mutterings of a subterranean chuckle.

Carr seemed slightly worried. He scowled at the tip of his cigar, but kept his lips rigidly clamped shut.

"Go ahead," Selby said.

"Naturally it occurred to me, too, that Grolley might die before we got a settlement out of him. I thought, 'Now wouldn't it be just too bad if I put up a lot of money and we worked things out so we were on the verge of getting a property settlement, and Grolley should up and die.' Of course it would be a windfall to Mrs. Grolley, but that would leave me out in the cold. So I provided against that."

"How?" Selby asked.

"She made an assignment of a part of her expectancy to me, and she made a will in my favor, leaving me a sum equal to that which would go to her daughter and making me the guardian of the daughter—to be good for thirty days after her husband's death."

"In other words," Selby said, "if the daughter got half of Grolley's estate, you were to get the other half under Mrs. Grolley's will?"

"That's right. . . . That, mind you, was in case Mrs. Grolley died before the settlement was completed. She thought that a will of that sort would keep me interested in protecting the child's interests—as indeed it would.

"In the event Grolley died before the settlement was made, then Mrs. Grolley was to give me one-half of her interest in the estate. . . . Get the point? If her husband died, and she survived him, I was to get one-quarter of the estate, on the theory that one-half would go to the child and one-half to her. I'd have a half of her half, or one-quarter."

"And if she died within the thirty-day limit, you'd get *all* of her share?" Selby asked.

Teel beamed. "That's it, my boy. That's it exactly. That's the way Jackson C. Teel protected himself."

"It gives you quite an interest in the estate," Selby said.

"It does for a fact," Teel admitted, and then added significantly, *"I planned it that way,"* and burst into booming laughter.

"You stood to profit by Mrs. Grolley's death."

"That's right," Teel agreed readily. "No use quarreling with simple arithmetic. I didn't kill her; but whoever did put money in my pocket—the difference between a quarter and a half of whatever Grolley left."

"Suppose," Selby asked, "Grolley left a will disinheriting his wife and child?"

"Fortunes of war," Teel said, "but don't think I'll

submit to anything like that tamely. I'll fight it through every court in the land, and when they fight Jackson C. Teel, they've got a fight on their hands. Never fight until you have to, that's my motto, and once you start fighting, see it through. Give them everything you have. Faint heart never won fair lady. When you start scrapping, wade right in and never stop."

Selby turned abruptly to Carr. "Did you make any search for a will in Grolley's house, Carr?"

It was apparent that the quick question caught the lawyer somewhat off his guard. Immersed in the part he was playing, it took him a moment to comprehend the full effect of Selby's question. "I'm not certain that I understand just what you're getting at, Selby."

"You were seen in the vicinity of Grolley's cabin with a woman wearing a light tan outfit with a pink blouse. The woman had a baby with her."

"When?" Carr asked.

"Thursday morning."

Carr's frown was the unconscious reflex of a man trying his best to concentrate. "Oh," he said, his face lighting up, "I know what you mean. I saw Mrs. Grolley very briefly Thursday morning. I had learned that her husband was in the hospital. We didn't deem it advisable to see him until he had more fully recovered. I explained to her, however, that she would have to make certain adjustments in her outlook, so far as her husband was concerned. She'd known him as a man who was clean and fairly well dressed. I drove her past the place where Grolley lived so she could see the shack."

"And you didn't go in?" Selby asked.

"No," Carr said promptly, "we didn't go in."

"Do you know anything about a will?"

"No. I don't think he left one. I'm virtually certain he didn't."

"What makes you so certain?"

"Letters which Grolley wrote to his wife."

"I believe you said you had those letters."

"That's right. I brought them with me. I thought you might like to look them over."

Carr opened a brief case, tossed a packet of letters on Selby's desk. Selby untied the string, saw the familiar backhanded chirography of Ezra Grolley on the envelope. He opened the letters one at a time and read them.

They were beyond doubt valuable as evidence. In them, in his stilted, impersonal phraseology, Grolley had admitted that he had made a poor husband, that he had abandoned and deserted his wife, that since the fault was all his, he intended to give her an allowance of ninety dollars per month—an amount which apparently seemed princely to the miserly recluse.

Another letter, dated some eleven months earlier, stated that Grolley had no relatives about whom he cared anything, that he had a sister somewhere, that he hadn't heard from her for years, that they never had been very close, and he saw no reason for letting her have any of his property. He intended to leave all his property to his wife unless, of course, he added cautiously, "something should happen to make me change my mind."

The amount of the estate, he went on to assure her, was not particularly large, but it would be something of a nest egg. He explained that it was hard to make money out of rabbits, what with feed as high as it was.

Selby had to smile at the manner in which Grolley, fearing that he had betrayed himself by mentioning that there would be a nest egg for his wife in the event he should pass away, had tried to cover up.

"Well?" Carr asked when Selby had finished reading the letters.

"Very interesting," Selby commented.

"Of course you understand that these letters will be evidence in any litigation which may arise concerning the estate."

"Naturally."

"I'm showing these to you simply to assist you in investigating a crime. I consider this evidence as strictly confidential. I wouldn't want you to tip off my hand."

"I understand."

Teel said, "Well, I suppose you'll want to know about how I learned there was enough property involved to make it worth my while, Mr. Selby."

Selby said, "Exactly. I was about to bring that up."

"I was satisfied you were. . . . Well, it's an interesting story. When a savings account lies dormant for a certain period of time, the custody is transferred to the state. It's necessary to go through a little red tape in that connection, and I'm the sharpshooter that watches the unwinding of that red tape. Whenever I see an inactive deposit worth anything at all, I get busy right away and investigate, and the purpose of that investigation, Selby, is to determine just what's in it for old Jackson C. Teel. When it comes to business matters, I'm not a philanthropist."

Carr said, "He isn't as black as he's painting himself, Selby. I've known him for some time. He's one of the most charitable men I know."

"Oh, *charities*," Teel said. "That's different. I sympathize with the unfortunate. I like to give to worthy causes. Frankly, Mr. Selby, I don't give a damn about keeping money after I get it. I gamble for the fun and the excitement. And that'll explain about that little girl, Selby. I'd like to see that she gets the breaks. That's philanthropy. Her mother knew the way I felt. That's why she nominated me as guardian in her will."

Carr said, "That will's been filed for probate, and I'm also filing an application for letters of guardianship of the person and estate of the minor."

Selby looked at Teel curiously. "I suppose you think there'd be nothing wrong in having a girl brought up in your form of life, Teel."

"Don't kid yourself," Teel said. "It's swell for me. It would be bad for a girl. No, sir. That girl will know her Uncle Jackson only as an eccentric investor. She'll be placed in the best schools money can buy. She'll never know just what sort of business I'm in."

"And suppose her own money isn't sufficient to pay the way?"

"Then Jackson C. Teel will keep putting money into the kitty. . . . What's the good of money if you can't do something with it?"

Selby tried another tack. "Have you," he asked, "any definite idea as to the exact size of Grolley's estate?"

Teel's face set instantly into a frozen fixity of expression. It was as though he had been sitting in a poker game and had just been dealt a straight flush.

"No," he said, and Selby had the distinct impression he was lying.

Selby said, "Don't take offense, but I'd like to know what you were doing Thursday—say between eleven and two."

Carr leaned forward, as though to expostulate. Teel waved him into silence. "Thursday," he mumbled, "between eleven and— Oh, yes, I was having my picture taken."

"Where?"

"Wingate's Studio."

"Over what period of time?"

Teel chuckled. "From eleven o'clock until four-thirty. You probably know old Wingate. As long as a subject will sit for him, he'll really go to town. He said I had a perfect face for camera portrayal, got me into his darkroom while he developed his negatives, and then dried the negatives in—alcohol, I guess it was—printed proofs, didn't like what he'd done and had me sit all over again. Got to talking, and pulled out about half of his collection to show me. He's a gabby cuss, but interesting—and he's an artist."

"You were there all that time?"

"That's right. My appointment was for eleven, and I hit it right on the nose. I didn't have anything else to do, so I sat around. . . . Guess a man's a conceited animal. I like to see my own face portrayed in the best way—most flattering way, I should say. Wingate dates his negatives. He'll remember all about it."

The telephone rang sharply. Selby picked up the receiver, and Mrs. Brandon said, "Doug, do you know where my husband is?"

"No. Why? Is something the matter?"

"Yes."

"You've tried the office, of course?"

"Yes. They thought he was with you. He said when he left that he was going to see you."

"He'll probably get in touch with me, then. What shall I tell him?"

"Tell him I want to see him right away—both of you."

"Something the matter?"

"Yes."

"Something you can tell me over the telephone?"

"No. Have him call me please, as soon as he comes in."

Selby hung up the telephone. Teel exchanged glances with Carr. "Well," Teel said, "you're a busy man, Mr. Selby. I guess I've given you all the assistance I can. If there's anything you want to ask me at any time, just call on me."

Selby, worried at the note which had been in Mrs.

Brandon's voice, and anxious to clear the decks, got to his feet. "Thank you," he said.

They shook hands with Selby, Teel with genial cordiality, Carr with grave dignity. At the door, Teel turned back. "*Anything* you want," he said, "get in touch with me. Don't ask Carr, because he's secretive. Ask me. I put my cards on the table."

Carr managed to hold himself somewhat aloof without seeming in the least to be conscious of the fact. It was as though he were registering disapproval of his client's actions, and Selby, knowing that the entire affair had been carefully rehearsed to give him just that impression, watched their exit with eyes in which there was the trace of a smile.

13

AS SOON AS THEY HAD LEFT, SELBY STARTED TRYING TO locate Brandon on the telephone. He was putting through his third call when Brandon himself walked into the office.

Selby said, "Call your wife at once, Rex."

The sheriff glanced at him sharply. "Something the matter?"

"I think so."

Brandon said, "Otto Larkin's on his way up here, Doug. I need a minute to talk with you before we have any interruptions."

"I think Mrs. Brandon's call was urgent," Selby said, motioning toward the telephone.

Brandon picked up the telephone, said to the courthouse operator, "This is Sheriff Brandon. Get me my house, will you?" then, holding his hand cupped over the mouthpiece, said to Selby, while he waited with the receiver at his ear, "Otto Larkin thinks we're holding out on him. I told him nothing of the sort. He's on his way up here to get wised up. I told him we'd give him all the facts we had."

Selby said, "This crime doesn't concern him. It wasn't committed in the city limits."

"I know, but he thinks the criminals reside in the city limits, and that if Mrs. Grolley was forced into a car near the bus depot it brings it within his jurisdiction. . . . You can't argue against that, Doug."

"No," Selby admitted, "but you know what he wants. He'll pump us for information and then spread it around where it will do the most harm."

"I know, but—" Brandon broke off to take his hand away from the mouthpiece of the telephone. "Hello. Yes, this is Rex. What is it?"

The sheriff listened for several moments, then said sharply, "When?" Then after an interval of silence, he said, "Doug and I have an appointment with Otto Larkin. Just as soon as we're finished—" He broke off as a knock sounded on the outer door of Selby's private office.

Selby, pushing back his chair, said irritably, "He wouldn't go around through the outer office and be announced. Not Larkin."

Brandon said into the telephone, "He's at the door

now. I'll have to let this go until we can get rid of him. Doug and I will come out just as soon as we're finished."

Brandon dropped the receiver back into place as Selby opened the door to the pompous chief of police.

"Hello, Doug. I was talking with Rex a few minutes ago, and told him I thought you fellows were holding out on me."

"Come in," Selby said. "Have a chair. What gave you that idea?"

"You're not keeping me posted on what's going on. After all, the killer is right here in Madison City. If you boys want to get him, we'll all have to co-operate."

"Sounds reasonable," Selby said, walking back to the swivel chair behind the desk.

"Well, you haven't given me very much to work on."

"*We* haven't very much to work on ourselves."

"What's this about a lot of money being taken from the shack?"

"I don't know. Someone got in Saturday night, went through the place pretty thoroughly, even tore up the floor. There's a hole in the ground, under the floor, and just about under the bed."

"I saw that hole," Larkin interrupted. "It was lined with gunny sacks. Looks as though there'd been some coin bags in there."

"There may have been," Selby admitted.

"What else did you find?" Larkin asked.

"A will," Selby said.

Larkin sat bolt upright. "You mean Ezra Grolley left a will that was found there in that hole?"

"That's right."

"Where is it now?"

"I don't happen to have it here right now, but I expect to have it by tomorrow morning."

"What did it say?"

"Simply that he left all of his property to his sister. The will was dated in nineteen hundred and thirty-five."

"What do you know about that?" Larkin said, fumbling awkwardly in his pocket for cigarettes. "Burnt my right hand—bad blister," he explained. "Right where it hurts most when I try to use my fingers."

Selby pushed a humidor across to him. "Here. Try one of these."

Larkin reached for the cigar, looked at the brand, clipped off the end, lit up, and settled back in his chair with every indication of intending that his visit should last the cigar out.

Selby said, "Carr showed me some correspondence—letters which Ezra Grolley had written to his wife. There's nothing in there which would serve as a clue."

"What's this about his knowing nothing about the baby?" Larkin asked.

"I'm not certain about that," Selby said. "I think he knew there was a possibility that there might be issue of his marriage. I think he was really an ingrained old bachelor. I think that Mrs. Grolley thought it would be a lot better all around to wait until she was able to travel, and then let Grolley see his daughter."

"Hell of a note," Larkin muttered through cigar smoke.

"We must remember that Grolley was rather a peculiar kettle of fish," Selby pointed out.

"What other clues have you got?"

"That's about all," Selby said, "except we're able to fix the time of the murder rather exactly between eleven-forty and twelve-fifty Thursday."

Larkin said, "That's good. It gives us something to work on. What was Mrs. Lossten doing then?"

"I don't know," Selby said. "I have been unable to reach Mrs. Lossten."

"Why?"

"Apparently she's hiding."

Larkin's eyes glittered. "You going to let her get away with that?"

"I understand," Selby went on, "that she's hiding from the service of a subpoena. Her attorney feels that

A. B. Carr wants to get her on the stand and turn her inside out before she knows just what Carr is planning."

"Her lawyer's Inez Stapleton?"

"Yes."

"Did you get that information straight?" Larkin asked.

"Yes."

"From Inez?"

Selby hesitated a moment, then nodded.

"Checked up on anybody else?" the chief asked.

"Jackson Teel," Selby said. "He's the one who was backing Mrs. Grolley."

"What was he doing?"

"Having his picture taken at Wingate's gallery. We haven't checked up on it yet, but it sounds ironclad."

"How do you know, if you haven't checked up?"

"Because it's something which can be verified. If we start checking up and it doesn't pan out, Teel has put himself right out on the end of a limb. If it does check, it will be an absolute alibi."

"Where's that will now?"

Selby said, "It's being checked for evidence."

"What sort of evidence?"

"Fingerprints, in part."

"And some effort being made to show whether it's genuine or not?"

"That's right. Stone, the handwriting expert, has it."

"Well," Larkin said, "I'm sort of running around in circles without knowing what's going on. You boys should keep me posted."

"If you want to do something," Selby said, "get Mrs. Lossten and her husband, find out where they are, and bring them in."

"You said *bring*?"

"That's right."

The chief of police promptly got to his feet. "Well now," he said, "*that's* something I can sink my teeth into. I'll find them and bring them in, all right."

Selby said, "Of course, we don't want to go *too* strong until we know more definitely what we're doing."

"What about those automobile tracks out at the place where the murder was committed?" Larkin asked. "I understand they fit the tracks of that Lossten car."

Selby said, "The Lossten car had a Skidless tire on the left front. Mrs. Lossten's testimony at the inquest *indicated* the car was never out of her possession after she found it on Thursday morning except for the time the police had it. The police had finished with it by eleven o'clock. I want to get her to say that again."

Larkin said, "That's a pretty good case of circumstantial evidence right there."

"It creates a suspicion," Selby admitted.

173

"Well, what more do you want?"

"Proof."

Larkin said, "The way you get proof is by rounding up the suspicious characters and tearing them apart."

"That's true enough," Selby admitted, "but when you do that, you want to have enough on them to check their stories."

"Well, I don't know. People are beginning to ask questions about this case. When they see people coming and going from the D.A.'s office, it makes 'em feel things are being done. . . . Makes the newspapers feel good, too. They like to have things to write about. . . . How Mrs. Blank looked while waiting to be questioned, and that sort of stuff."

Selby said, "If it doesn't help solve the case, it doesn't get you anywhere in the long run. . . . We hate to cut this short, Larkin, but Rex and I have some people waiting to talk with us."

Larkin heaved his weight up out of the chair. "Well, I'll get busy," he promised with glib cordiality.

They were silent while Larkin walked importantly to the door.

"Of course," Selby said as Larkin opened the door, "all of this is in strict confidence."

"Oh, sure," Larkin agreed, and walked out into the corridor, closing the door behind him. Brandon looked at Selby. "He's aiming to double-cross us right now. You're too generous, Doug."

"Didn't you want me to tell him the facts?"

"Well, you put your cards right on the table. You didn't hold anything back."

"What did you expect me to do? I couldn't lie to him."

"Well," Brandon said, scratching the back of his head thoughtfully, "if I'd been doing it, I'd have beat around the bush a lot more."

"What did Mrs. Brandon want?" Selby asked.

The sheriff got up out of his chair, stood looking toward the door of Selby's office. "We've got to go out to see her. I want to wait until Larkin has got out of the courthouse before we leave. Otherwise he'll smell a rat."

"What rat is there to smell?" Selby asked.

"Carr has been doing some funny stuff. I've never seen the missus quite so worked up. I'm afraid we've got a job on our hands."

"Doing what?" Selby asked.

"Apparently busting Mrs. Grolley's will. I don't see no other way out of it."

"Why?"

"Mrs. Grolley nominated this man, Teel, as the guardian of her little girl."

"And Mrs. Brandon doesn't like it?" Selby asked, grinning.

The sheriff said, "You come along with me, Doug Selby, and you'll find out what she thinks about it."

14

MRS. BRANDON MET THEM AT THE DOOR. ABOUT HER was an ominous calm. She said, "You come in here, both of you. I want to show you something."

She took them through the living room and dining room into the kitchen where the baby lay in its bassinet. On the kitchen table was a folded legal document. "Look at this," she said, handing it to Selby.

Brandon read over Selby's shoulder.

Selby said, "This is a notice, Mrs. Brandon, ordering you to appear and show cause why Jackson C. Teel shouldn't be appointed guardian of the person and estate of Ruth Winifred Grolley in accordance with the application for letters of guardianship, a copy of which is attached hereto. . . . You'll notice that Teel has made the application for guardianship based on a nomination and appointment by the mother contained in her will."

"Who's Teel?" Mrs. Brandon asked.

"I've just been talking with him," Selby said.

"Well, who is he?"

"He's a person who befriended Mrs. Grolley. He financed her action against her husband—or was ready to do so. He arranged for Carr to act as her attorney."

"Just what I thought," Mrs. Brandon said with something of a snort. "He's one of Carr's henchmen, one of that ilk! Now you listen to me, Doug Selby, and you too, Rex Brandon. Don't start quoting me any law. I don't care what the law is. This is a sweet little baby girl, and A. B. Carr or any of his associates aren't fit persons to have anything to do with her. This little baby has inherited a sizeable fortune. If it's carefully handled by someone who has her interests at heart, she's going to be educated with it and have a nest egg which will make her as popular with the boys as a honey jar with a mess of flies. . . . But you let that crook-coddling, hell-raising, gambling outfit get hold of that money, and it'll be gone."

"Now don't get all riled up, Ma," Brandon said reassuringly. "The court looks after things like that. It makes a guardian put up a bond, and makes him account—"

"There you go," she interrupted, "telling me what

the law is. Old A.B.C. will find a dozen different loop-holes in the law."

"He can't," Brandon said. "The judge will see to that."

"Shucks. He'll razzledazzle that money right out from under the judge's eyes. He'll board her with some dummy, and charge a fancy price, but the little girl won't get anything except the cheapest kind of food and care. He'll charge fees for the guardian, and old A.B.C. himself will scare up lawsuits that have to be defended by him at so much per. . . . And what's more, I don't want her brought up in that atmosphere. I'll keep her myself before I'll let her go to people like that."

"But, Ma," Brandon pointed out, "you can't keep her. You ain't related to her. You haven't any claim on her."

"Don't you think I haven't," she said, facing him angrily. "I've got her, haven't I?"

"You're just keeping her."

"You bet I'm keeping her!"

Brandon turned to Selby for moral backing. "Doug can tell you what the law is. Mrs. Grolley made a will in case anything happened to her—"

"She made that will because this man Teel *told* her to make it," Mrs. Brandon snapped. "Now, Doug Selby, you're a lawyer. You get busy and see that the judge understands the circumstances. See that that will doesn't stand up. I'm not going to have this man Teel appointed guardian, and that's all there is to it."

"But we're hardly in a position to contest the will," Selby said. "We—"

"I don't want any of your excuses, Doug Selby. I've teamed along with both of you through lots of tough sledding, and this is the first time you've heard a peep out of me. But if you two can't find some way of keeping a shyster and his gang from getting control of this child, you'd better resign from office and tell the taxpayers the job was just too big for you. . . . Now then, I'm going to cook supper, and you're going to be here for supper, Doug Selby. You two men get out of the kitchen and figure out what you're going to do. I don't care what it is, but understand one thing. That baby stays right here until I find someone to take it who can be trusted. And I ain't so certain but I'll raise her myself."

"I reckon," the sheriff said to Selby, "that's our exit line."

Selby started from the kitchen. Brandon, halfway to the door, turned around to say, "Listen, Ma, you can't keep her with you always. You're getting pretty attached to her, I know, but she makes a lot of extra work and—"

"You just forget about the work," Mrs. Brandon cut in, "and don't think you're going to talk me out of this either, Rex Brandon. Any time a big, healthy woman like me can't take one baby to raise without upsetting everything, there's something wrong somewhere. Land sakes, my mother raised eight of us, and did the cooking for a couple of hired men, along with plenty of other things. And there weren't any washing machines and electricity and vacuum cleaners and electric irons those days. When women worked, they worked. . . . What are you talking about, can't take care of this baby! Now get along, both of you. Start figuring what *you're* going to do, and leave this end of it to me."

Brandon and Selby walked out on the cool, vine-covered porch. The sheriff fished the cloth tobacco sack from his pocket. Selby reached for his pipe.

"I feel like a kid who's thrown a baseball through a window," Selby said.

The men scraped matches into flame and lit up.

"Well, Doug," the sheriff said, "I don't know how you're going to do it."

Selby puffed thoughtfully at his pipe. "There isn't any way. The mother had the right to nominate a guardian in her will. . . . Of course, we could try to show Teel isn't a proper person to have the guardianship of the child, but that's going to be quite an order."

"It may be quite an order," Brandon said, "but we've got it."

"In my capacity as district attorney, I can't very well do that," Selby said.

"Well," Brandon announced, "in my capacity as the nominal head of this household, I can't live here no longer if you don't do it, Doug."

Selby said, "We'll wire the San Francisco police and see what they can find out about Teel. We may unearth something there."

"Got any other plans?" the sheriff asked.

"Not yet."

"Well, son, we got our orders."

The district attorney chuckled. "We sure did," he admitted.

The telephone rang while the men were sitting smoking on the porch. Brandon, answering it, said, "It's for you, Doug. Long distance calling."

Selby took the telephone. It was Sydney Bell Stone on the line. He said, "Just wanted to let you know, Mr. Selby, that the will is a forgery."

"You're sure?"

"Absolutely. I have measured the exact color changes in the ink with my tintometer. I have placed the document in a specially constructed vault where conditions exist which expedite the process of ink oxidization. By recording those changes, I have concluded the ink on the document is less than a week old."

"How about the letter?"

"The letter is also a forgery. They're both the work of a professional forger."

"What do you mean by that?" Selby asked.

"I mean that ordinarily when we find family documents, such as a will, to be forgery, we are dealing with a rank amateur, who feels aggrieved because the relative didn't leave the kind of a will he wanted. So forgery is resorted to in an attempt to remedy the situation. But the forger has had no previous practice, and, therefore but little skill.

"This case, however, is different. I think we have here the work of a very clever expert. Were it not for the fact that this person has probably failed to keep abreast of modern, scientific methods of detection, the will might well have been declared genuine. . . . I'm emphasizing this because, as I understand it, you're interested in the criminal aspect of the case, not in who gets the estate."

"In a way, that's right," Selby said. "Suppose you bring the documents to Madison City. There's another will which I want you to study carefully."

"Where is it?"

"In the County Clerk's office," Selby said. "The will of Alice Grolley. If we're dealing with forgeries, we'd better make a thorough investigation."

"I'll be there at ten o'clock tomorrow morning," Stone promised, "and have these documents with me."

Selby hung up, went back to the porch and reported the conversation to Brandon, then sat smoking for several silent minutes.

At length he straightened. "Let's go call the San Francisco police, Rex. I'd like to find out if there are any forgeries in Teel's past record."

"Why should he forge a will in favor of someone else?" Brandon asked.

"Because," Selby pointed out, "it would be a final artistic touch. If Carr could get Grolley's sister into court, relying on a will which he could prove was a forgery, people would lose all sympathy with her. They'd brand her as a complete fraud. Carr's client would then have easy sailing."

Brandon scratched his head. "You're right there," he said. "It might be just as well, son, if we had the San Francisco police workin' on Teel's record before we came back for supper."

15

SYLVIA MARTIN DROPPED IN TO SEE SELBY LESS THAN
ten minutes after he had put through a call to the San
Francisco police.

"Doug," she asked, "how much did you tell Otto
Larkin?"

"Not too much," Selby said. "Why?"

"He's double-crossing you."

"That's nothing new."

"He's double-crossing you this time in a big way.
You don't suppose he's been able to slip in ahead of
you and solve the murder, do you?"

"If he has, he's a better man than I am," Selby said.

"Doug, are you laying off the Losstens?"

"No. Why should I?"

"There's talk around town that you are."

"Why should I?"

She averted her eyes and said, "I knew you weren't.

. . . Doug, just how much evidence is there against them?"

"I don't know. There's some circumstantial evidence —and that automobile of theirs seems to have figured in the case altogether too prominently."

"You've checked up on the tires?"

"Yes. It looks very much as though that car had been out to the Glencannon Ranch."

"And the car was in the Losstens' hands from noon on Thursday?"

"That's right. At least her testimony indicates as much."

"Doesn't that give you a case?"

"Not by itself."

"Why?"

"Because of lots of things, Sylvia."

"Then you think there's some other car with a Skidless tire on the left front that also enters into the case?"

"Perhaps, but here's a possibility which apparently hasn't been given careful consideration. . . . Suppose there had to be some preliminary preparations for the kidnaping of Mrs. Grolley made the night before? And then again, let's suppose Old A. B. Carr wasn't just making a grandstand when he made that accusation at the inquest. *Suppose the person who was driving that car tried to kill Mrs. Grolley and got Mrs. Hunter and her baby by mistake.* I don't know whether you've noticed it, but there's a strong resemblance between the two women. Aside from a difference in complexion, they're just about the same height, age, and build."

Sylvia shook her head. "You can't do it, Doug."

"Can't do what?"

"Play around with that supposition of A. B. Carr's —not unless there's some very definite proof of it."

"Why?"

"Oh, can't you see? People are saying already that it's because of—well, because of a personal friendship that you don't arrest Mrs. Lossten."

"Because of Inez Stapleton?" Selby asked.

Sylvia Martin nodded her head quickly. "Look, let's talk about something else. I'm not ready to talk about the case now. I don't know enough about it. I just wanted to tell you that Larkin is double-crossing you.— The *Blade* will be off the press about now. I wanted to be with you when it hit the streets."

"And get some ammunition to fire back at them in tomorrow's *Clarion?*"

She nodded.

Selby patted her shoulder. "Good girl. You always show up when you think the going is getting tough. . . . You don't know the half of it this time."

"What is it, Doug?"

"Mrs. Brandon has given us an ultimatum to see that Teel doesn't get the guardianship of the Grolley baby."

"I thought that might happen," Sylvia said. "It's all right, of course, if you don't let it appear you're—well, trying to use your office to do it. You know Carr is clever when it comes to handling a situation like that."

"Don't I know it," Selby said, standing at the window looking down at the street. "He— Well, here comes the delivery boy with the *Blade*, Sylvia. We'll see what he has to say."

Sylvia Martin opened her purse, lit a cigarette. "Of course, Doug, it may be just a false alarm, but somehow I don't think so."

"Sydney Bell Stone rang up a little while ago," Selby said, "and reported on that will. . . . It's a forgery."

"He's absolutely certain?"

"Yes. That is, he can prove that it was written within the last two weeks."

"Did you tell Larkin?"

"No, but I told him I'd given the will to Stone for examination."

"You shouldn't have done it."

"Why?"

"Couldn't he telephone Stone, say he was police chief, and get the facts?"

"Possibly, but I had to tell him."

Sylvia laughed nervously. "I suspect him of all sorts of things. He certainly is trying to cut your throat."

"But if I hadn't told him, he'd have claimed I was holding out on him."

"Hold out on him, then," she said bitterly. "It's the only way to do with him. Let him get his own clues."

"After all, Sylvia, this isn't a *game* we're playing. We're trying to enforce law."

She started to say something, then checked herself. They smoked in silence for a moment until they heard steps in the corridor, and a newspaper was slid under the crack of Selby's door. He crossed over and picked it up.

Headlines streaming across the page carried the news, "CHIEF LARKIN CLOSES NET ON KILLER."

Selby and Sylvia Martin seated themselves side by side on the edge of the district attorney's desk and read the account which started with opening paragraphs well calculated to enhance the importance of the chief of police and belittle Selby and Brandon.

"While county officials, more experienced in erecting political fences than in actual police work, were floundering about trying to untangle the confused skein of events leading to the murder of Mrs. Ezra Grolley, Otto Larkin, Madison City's efficient chief of police, was quietly sawing wood.

"County officials, taking only such bits of evidence as have been dropped in their laps, and not knowing where or how to look for new evidence, have been hopelessly bewildered by the peculiar series of events which culminated in the murder of Mrs. Ezra Grolley. Larkin, backed by years of experience in criminal matters, knew how to look and when to look, to uncover new evidence.

"When county officials found a will in an excavation under the floor of Grolley's cabin, Larkin immediately came to the conclusion that the will was a forgery. Late this afternoon he talked over the telephone with Sydney Bell Stone, the famous handwriting expert and examiner of questioned documents. The chief of police suggested to Stone that it would be a good idea to test the ink for age. The expert communicated to Chief Larkin the result of this test. The will, which purports to have been dated in nineteen hundred and thirty-five and leaves all of the property to Sadie G. Lossten, was actually written within the last two weeks. It is, therefore, a forgery.

"A. B. Carr, veteran criminal attorney, suggested at the inquest on the Hunter baby in the hit-and-run case that there might well be a connection with the disappearance of Mrs. Grolley. The county officials pooh-poohed this suggestion. Larkin had been working on such a theory, however, even before Carr advanced it.

"Quietly but diligently he has been interviewing witnesses for days, asking questions here and there, visiting the all-night restaurants, trying to find if anyone noticed a car with a Louisiana license plate parked near his establishment.

"At last his efforts were rewarded. Larkin found evidence which indicates a most startling connection between the hit-and-run case and the death of Mrs. Grolley. John B. Train, who for years was a resident of New Orleans, happened to notice a car with Louisiana license plates.

"Train, who works as caretaker at a social club, had stopped in at the Okay Restaurant to get a sandwich and cup of coffee before retiring. He fixes the time as approximately one-thirty a.m. Thursday morning. There can be no doubt that the automobile he saw was the one which Mr. and Mrs. Lossten so stoutly maintain had been stolen. Among other things he noticed that the left front fender was crumpled as though it had recently been in an accident. He also noticed a triangular segment of glass broken off in the left rear window of the automobile. Upon being shown the Lossten automobile, he says there's absolutely no question but what that was the car.

"Comes now the startling fact that the car stopped in front of the telephone office and a young woman jumped out of the door to enter the telephone booth.

"That woman was Mrs. Ezra Grolley.

"Train noticed her particularly, noticed that she was wearing a light tan jacket and skirt. The collar of a pink blouse was visible at the neck. But what particularly attracted his attention was the fact that the woman was carrying a baby, and that the baby was crying fitfully. Train thought it unusual for a woman to be abroad at that hour of the night with a child so young, and concluded that the infant was sick and the mother was probably telephoning to the doctor.

"Train had all but dismissed the matter from his mind, and did not connect it with the hit-and-run case until Larkin, conducting his painstaking examination, questioned him.

"Larkin promptly subjected the Lossten automobile to a more thorough search than had been made by the county officials. Tucked in the back of the glove compartment, he found a pair of light brown gloves. Larkin noticed that Mrs. Lossten habitually wore dark clothes and black gloves. An examination of the light brown gloves disclosed the mark of a cleaning establishment in San Francisco where further investigation resulted in uncovering the fact that these gloves were the property of Mrs. Ezra Grolley, or, as she was known in San Francisco, of Alice Grolley. The mark which appears on the inside of the gloves is a code mark used by the cleaner for the purpose of identifying the customer's apparel.

"It is reasonable to suppose that Mrs. Grolley thought she was riding with 'friends,' and that some attempt was to be made to kill her at that time. She evidently escaped—temporarily. Did she get into another car, and did the person driving the Lossten machine follow—only to mistake the Hunter car for the one he wanted—after seeing a woman and baby riding in the machine?

"Larkin quietly went about getting the fingerprints of Terry Lossten. From them he was able to learn that Lossten was at one time convicted of forgery and served a five-year sentence in an eastern penitentiary. The fact that he has paid his debt to society would, of course, close the incident were it not for this new involvement.

"The *Blade* makes no specific accusations. We merely mention the facts which have been uncovered by Chief Larkin. The sheriff and the district attorney *should* know what to do with these facts. The *Blade* thinks its readers will know what they would want done. Certain it is that unless some drastic action is taken, there will be ample support for the rumors which have recently been whispered about the street—rumors to the effect that while it is sometimes easy to assume an attitude of rigid honesty so far as commercial bribes are concerned, there are more subtle considerations which are well calculated to rob the self-righteous 'crusader' of his efficiency.

"It is to be hoped that the county officials will take a lesson from Chief Larkin's unselfish devotion to duty and permit no petty official jealousies to keep them from availing themselves of the experience of Madison City's capable veteran chief of police.

"With such clues as the *Blade* is now able to place in the hands of the sheriff and the district attorney, it would certainly seem that an arrest should be made promptly and a conviction could be had with none of the spectacular beating of drums and fanfare of trumpets which has hitherto marked the routine handling of ordinary cases in the county offices."

Sylvia Martin's eyes were blazing with anger. "Of all the dirty, underhanded, despicable tricks," she said, "that's the lowest. . . . I suppose he learned about the will from you, then called the handwriting expert, and told him that he was working with you on the case, and so got the low-down."

"Probably," Selby said.

"The worst of it is," Sylvia Martin went on, "if that's true about Train, there's nothing we can do or say. . . . You know as well as I do, Doug Selby, that Larkin didn't go out and dig up that evidence. It was handed to him on a silver platter. Train hunted Larkin up and told him about seeing the car, then instead of getting in touch with you, Larkin held out on you."

Selby might not have heard her. His forehead creased in a frown, he was staring moodily at the carpet, puffing thoughtfully at his pipe.

"It's a dirty, underhanded, political knifing, Doug. Can't you do something?"

Selby said, "I have an idea, Sylvia, but in order to carry it out I've got to go into the gruesome."

"What do you mean?"

"I've got to go down to the Glencannon Ranch and reconstruct what happened when Mrs. Grolley was murdered. In order to do that, I'm going to have to follow every step Mrs. Grolley took as indicated by the trail of blood drops on the floor. . . . It isn't going to be pleasant—particularly as I'm going to stop at the slaughterhouse, get a pint of fresh blood, a medicine dropper, and conduct some experiments."

"On the track of something?" she asked.

He nodded.

"What?"

"Time enough to tell you when I see if it works. . . . And here's something else I wish you'd do, Sylvia. I want you to put two things in the paper, and have them fairly well separated."

"What are they?"

"First, in an interview with me, you have learned that, in my opinion, all of Grolley's estate has not as yet been recovered, that a relatively large sum of cash was in his hands about ten days before his death, and this cash has not as yet been found."

"What's the other thing?"

"And somewhere, in another part of the paper, comment on the human side of Grolley's character, mention how industrious he was, state that, according to neighbors, he would be up at the crack of dawn; that shortly before his death, one of the neighbors actually saw him spading trees in the northwest corner of his ranch by lantern light. He saw the light cast by the lantern, heard the clink of bits of gravel against the blade of the shovel, and thought someone was trying to steal irrigating water. He went out far enough to see that it was Grolley working away industriously by lantern light, spading up the ground under the trees."

Sylvia Martin's eyes glistened. "You mean you're baiting a trap, Doug, to see who comes and digs in that corner of the orchard?"

Selby nodded.

"But isn't it rather obvious—crude?"

"I want to be crude," Selby said. "Greed knows no finesse."

While the telephone had not been disconnected in the Glencannon bungalow, the lights had been shut off, and it was necessary for Selby to do his work by the aid of the flashlight which Sylvia Martin held.

With a pint container immersed in warm water to keep it at the proper temperature, Selby conducted his experiments using a medicine dropper. The first drop was released some eighteen inches from the floor.

"You can see," Selby said, "what happens. The little side-spray drops are barely noticeable. Now I'll keep raising the height at which the drop is released until we get just about the same degree of spatter-stain as in the case of those other drops."

Sylvia watched him as he gradually raised the medicine dropper until it was on a level with his head.

"That's about it, Doug," she said.

Selby nodded.

"But I don't see what you're trying to prove. It's certain that the blood came from the wound in her head."

"I wanted to make certain, that's all," Selby said absently. As he crossed the room he thoughtfully squeezed the last few drops of blood out of the dropper. Still in a brown study, he examined those last few drops carefully.

In the bathroom Selby disposed of the blood and washed out the container. Sylvia Martin, watching him, said abruptly, "Doug, don't fall for that hokum about the forged will. . . . Carr stole the original will and substituted the forgery."

Selby said, "No lawyer knew anything about that will—neither Carr nor Inez Stapleton."

"What do you mean?"

"Under our probate code, when a man marries after he makes a will, the will is deemed to be revoked insofar as the wife is concerned, and when a child is born after a will is made, the will is deemed revoked as to the child."

"Then it doesn't make any difference whether the will is forged or not?"

"Not so far as the property is concerned."

"You think that—that the attorneys for both sides knew that?"

"They should have. . . . Let's go."

Sylvia Martin remained silent. Nor did Selby make any further statement until they drove up in front of the *Clarion* office. Then he said, "Don't forget to put those two things in the paper, Sylvia, about the additional money and about his working in the orchard."

She placed her hand on his arm. "Don't worry. I won't. And remember, no matter what happens, I'm betting on you."

In front of the house where he roomed, Selby found Inez Stapleton seated in her parked automobile. She had evidently been waiting for some time.

"I *had* to see you, Doug," she said.

"Over the disclosures in the *Blade?*"

"Yes. I think that's the most despicable, cowardly thing I ever read in my life. What's more, it's a libel on my clients."

"Going to do anything about it?"

"I'm not certain that I can, Doug. I'm reading up on the law of libel."

"Where are your clients now?"

As she turned to him, the light from the dash of her automobile showed sharp worry-lines on her face. "Doug, I don't know. I'm going to tell you the whole thing. I had them under cover to avoid A.B.C.'s subpoena. I told them to drive up that mountain cutoff to the inn at Santa Rosalita, to register under their own names so there couldn't be any claim they'd resorted to flight on a criminal charge. . . . Well, Doug, they aren't there. They never went there."

Selby said, "I warned you what would happen, Inez."

"I know you did."

"Otto Larkin is looking for them. If he gets them, he's going to make the arrest and then dump the case in my lap. . . . You've done some talking about how I might cook my goose if I didn't quit being friendly with Carr. Well, you know what they're saying now?"

"That you aren't prosecuting because—because of me?"

"Yes."

"Doug, I'm sorry."

"It's done," he said. "No use getting steamed up about it. Did you know that they had had Mrs. Grolley in the car with them?"

"No. That's news to me. They insisted they went to bed and to sleep, that someone had stolen the car."

"It may be true."

She said, "I feel like an awful heel about this."

"You don't need to. You're a lawyer doing your duty by your clients. I'm a lawyer, and I'm going to do my duty by my client."

"Is that," she asked, "a declaration of war?"

Selby grinned at her. "No, of independence."

She laughed then, a quick, nervous laugh which seemed to catch midway in her throat. "I just wanted you to know," she said, starting the motor of her automobile. "I couldn't have slept if I'd thought you felt I'd double-crossed you."

"I didn't," he told her. "I knew better."

Her smile served only to etch the worry-lines deeper. " 'Night, Doug. I'm still going to fight for my clients."

Selby chuckled. "Better find 'em first. 'Night, Inez."

He stood watching her turn the car, saw the red glow of the taillight recede in the distance, then he went upstairs and to bed.

16

SYDNEY BELL STONE SET UP AN IMPROMPTU LABORATORY
in the clerk's office of the courthouse. He photographed
Mrs. Grolley's will and avoided questions asked him
by representatives of the newspapers. When he had finished, he came to Selby's office to make apologies.

"I'm afraid I walked into a trap yesterday. This
man telephoned, said he was the chief of police, and
that he'd been talking with you. I assumed he knew
all about our conversation."

"It's all right. Don't worry about it. What do you
think of that other will?"

"Too early to tell."

"How long will it take to get a definite opinion?"

"Probably a week."

"Hurry it up as much as you can."

"I will. I understand you recovered Mrs. Grolley's
purse."

"That's right."

"Was there a fountain pen in it?"

"Yes."

"It would help," Stone said, "to have that fountain pen."

"Could you tell if Mrs. Grolley's will was written with it?"

"I think so."

"It wouldn't have been in any event," Selby said. "The people with whom we are dealing are clever enough to have thought of that." But he took the expert down to the sheriff's office, got the fountain pen from Brandon's safe, and let him take a sample of the ink, a specimen of its writing, and a photograph of the point.

The day was one of hectic effort and little accomplishment. San Francisco police wired that Teel was just what he purported to be, a frequenter of the race track, a gambler, a money-broker, and a driver of hard business bargains, but so far as known a man who kept within the law.

Otto Larkin avoided Selby in person, but had the grace to try making a half-hearted explanation on the telephone. He had talked with a *Blade* reporter, and the reporter had "dressed things up," he explained. The newspaper had "tried to give him a boost." As for the other evidence on the automobile and the gloves, Larkin had intended to communicate that to the sheriff and the district attorney. "But you rushed me out of your office," he went on glibly, "before I had a chance to tell you about it. You remember you said you had some important people waiting. I figured I'd tell you later."

Selby listened silently, said, "I appreciate *just* how it is, Larkin," and hung up, thinking how much better open enmity was than hypocritical friendship.

The desert wind blew until nearly two o'clock in the afternoon, then died down abruptly. By sunset, the wind had shifted, and people were gazing hopefully at patches of drifting clouds, which darkened perceptibly with each hour.

Early dusk found Selby on the side road which led past the northwest corner of Grolley's property. Picking a place in an avocado tree which suited his purpose, he took some light supports from the back of his automobile, also some pieces of plyboard, and a coil of light rope. By the time it got too dark to work, he had a rude, fairly comfortable platform lashed to the branches of the tree. Sylvia Martin joined him as he was putting on the finishing touches, and Selby left her on watch while he moved their cars away to a safe distance. He rejoined her, carrying two powerful electric torches.

There was that about the environment which made

for silence between them as they watched the black shadows of night erase all objects on the ground, leaving only the tree branches silhouetted against the faint illumination of the cloudy heavens. Occasionally they could glimpse a star in between cloud edges. Then, later, there were no more stars. A faint breeze stirred the leaves, making an accompaniment for the little noises of the night. The clouds dropped lower, until the lights cast by Madison City showed on the cloud floor as a partially luminous patch of reddish visibility. The minutes, which at first had been filled with suspense, dragged into cramped hours. An automobile droned by, the lights cutting long pencils of brilliant illumination, then again all was silent.

"Don't you suppose we could chance one smoke, Doug?" Sylvia whispered.

"It looks as though we've drawn a blank anyway," Selby grumbled, fishing his pipe from his pocket. "I thought certain we'd get— Wait a minute. . . . Hold everything, Sylvia."

A faint light flickered over the ground below, then was extinguished.

They heard the sound of someone stumbling over rough ground, then the light again, this time very close. Leaning forward to peer down, they could see the vague form of a man silhouetted against the diffused illumination cast by an electric flashlight over the lens of which a doubled handkerchief had been tied.

The beam of the flashlight was directed down at the ground now, moving in quick, questing half circles, until it came to rest on the place where Selby had baited his trap by disturbing the earth just enough to make a change in color noticeable.

Almost immediately the man below them began to dig.

Afraid to move lest some creaking of their improvised platform should give the alarm, Selby and Sylvia Martin sat waiting, listening to the sounds of the shovel as it bit into the rich, loamy soil below the tree, hearing the hoarse, rapid breathing of the man below.

At length he stopped to rest. They heard the rustle of the cellophane around a cigarette pack. A match scraped into flame, and they saw the face of Terry B. Lossten etched into sharp brilliance by the match which was held in his cupped hand.

"Hold the flashlight when I drop, Sylvia," Selby whispered.

Lossten paused for a moment as though his ears had caught some vague, faint sound of the whisper, then he resumed his digging. As he did so, Selby slid off the edge of the platform, hung by his hands for a moment, then thudded to the ground.

The brilliant beam of the flashlight shot into the darkness just over Selby's head, catching the surprised figure of Lossten, holding him in sharp brilliance.

The little man instinctively raised his eyes and caught the dazzling beam full on his face. His cigarette dropped to the ground. Before he could more than fling up an arm to protect his eyes, Selby said, "Suppose we talk it over, Lossten."

He whirled toward the sound of the voice. His hands gripped the handle of the shovel, raised it as a weapon, holding the steel blade poised.

Selby said, "Don't try it. It wouldn't be healthy."

As Lossten stood poised and undecided, Sylvia Martin said calmly, "Drop that shovel, or I'll shoot."

The effect was instantaneous. Lossten dropped the shovel. His hands shot up in the air. "What is it?" he asked.

"What," Selby asked, "are you doing here?"

"Digging."

"What for?"

"That's my business."

"I'm afraid I'm going to have to take you into custody."

"What for?"

"To get you to answer questions."

Lossten, still blinded by the beam of light which held

him pilloried in a pitiless glare, said, "I get you now. You're the D.A."

"Right."

"Well, you've got nothing on me. This is my wife's property. I've got a right to dig here all I want. Get tough, and I can throw you off as a trespasser."

"That," Selby said, "is an idea."

Lossten showed his apprehension. "Who's that up there?" he asked, indicating the tree platform from which Sylvia was holding him in the beam of the flashlight.

"Oh, just some people," Selby said. "You don't happen to have a gun on you, do you, Lossten?"

"Not me. I never pack a rod."

"I take it you believe the pen is mightier than the sword."

Lossten said, "Sure, go ahead. Rub it in. Just because I did a term in stir for pen-pushing, you hicks have an idea you can frame anything on me."

Selby said, "Turn around. Keep your hands up. I'll verify that about the gun."

Lossten turned readily enough. Selby, watching him carefully, stepped up and ran his hands over the outlines of the man's clothes. When he found no weapon, he said, "Sit down, Lossten. We're going to talk," and to Sylvia, "Toss me that other flashlight, and then switch out the one you have."

Sylvia threw down the flashlight, and Selby, holding the big, five-cell torch in his hand, said, "Sit over there, away from the shovel, with your back against that tree, Lossten. That's better. You're hardly the fish I expected to catch on the hook I baited."

"No?"

"No. I was looking for someone else."

"Well, it was pretty good bait," Lossten said. "I didn't smell a rat until I heard you hit the ground. . . . Putting it in two places in the paper that way was what made me fall for it."

Selby said, "If you'd admit forging the will, you and I might get along a lot better."

"Stick my head in a noose, eh?" Lossten asked.

"We can prove it on you sooner or later."

"Go ahead and try."

"I'm interested in solving a murder, Lossten, not mixing into a will contest."

"That's what you say."

"Where were you between eleven-thirty in the morning and one o'clock in the afternoon on Thursday?"

"I don't know."

"You've read the papers?"

"Yes."

"You must appreciate the importance of knowing."

"It may be important, but I don't know where I was."

"Were you driving your car?"

"I may have been. We had it all Thursday afternoon."

"Anyone with you?"

"I wouldn't even remember that—not now."

"Where are you and your wife staying?"

Lossten said, "Now listen, Selby, you're a right guy. You're not like that big palooka of a police chief. I'd like to play ball with you. But right now we're up against a slick lawyer who's trying to gyp us out of our property. You start throwing your weight around, and you're not making it any easier for us."

Selby said, "I'll make you a sporting proposition, Lossten."

"What is it?"

"Go to the office of Inez Stapleton, your attorney. Stay there until I send for you, and we'll declare a recess on everything else."

Lossten took another cigarette from his pocket. Selby pushed tobacco down into his pipe, and up on the platform a match flared into flame as Sylvia Martin relieved the nervous tension with a welcome cigarette.

"Why so generous?" Lossten asked.

209

"Because," Selby said, "I'm gunning for other game."

"How do you know I won't skip out?"

"I don't."

"You're taking pretty big chances."

"No, I'm not, Lossten. You are."

"What do you mean?"

"I'm telling you in the presence of witnesses that I want to question you. I'm also telling you that I can take you down to the courthouse and lock you up. I don't want to do that. I want to give you a fair deal. I don't want to question you about the murder unless your lawyer is present. If you'll give me your word to go to her office and wait there until I come, I'll take your word and let you go."

"The word of an ex-con?"

"That's right. If you ran away, Lossten, you couldn't get very far, and the mere act of running would put a rope around your neck."

Lossten smoked for several silent seconds, then he said, "It's a deal. Do I start now?"

"You start now," Selby said.

"She won't be in her office."

"You can telephone her and get her there."

"How long do I wait?"

"Until two o'clock in the morning unless you hear from me before."

"That's a long while."

"It won't be any shorter in jail."

"It's a deal," Lossten said. He got to his feet, picked up his shovel, and switched on his flashlight. The doubled handkerchief gave a subdued, diffused illumination, a certain weird light which made the trees seem unnatural, black specters watching in grim rows.

"Well," Lossten said, "I'll be on my way."

"I don't suppose," Selby said, "you'd care to tell me how you managed to get all your information about things that are going on in Madison City."

"I sort of mix around. I'm a good listener."

"You knew that Grolley was married, and that his wife was coming to Madison City?"

Lossten paused for a moment to lean on his shovel. He said, "I'm in a spot. They're trying to make Sadie and me the goats. . . . I was a pen-pusher once, and a good one. I did my time in stir and got a clean bill of health—as much as they can give you when you get out of the big house. But with that record of mine, all they need is just a little evidence, and they could frame a murder rap on me. I've seen those things done lots of times. When I read the paper tonight, I decided there was a bunch of jack out here, and that it was ours. So I came after it. That's the low-down. I didn't croak that girl and neither did Sadie. But that lawyer is out to frame us, and you've got enough to rig us if you're crooked. *I* think you're square. I'm willing to play ball—but all you have is my word for it. Now then, does your offer still hold, or are you going to take me to the hoosegow?"

"The offer still holds."

Lossten picked up his shovel. "See you later," he said, and started trudging away through the trees.

Selby stood waiting until the sound of Lossten's steps had disappeared, until there was no longer any suggestion of the weird patch of light which emanated from his shrouded flashlight.

"Now what do we do?" Sylvia asked, sliding down out of the tree.

Selby stood thoughtfully staring down at the hole Lossten had dug. "We make a complete about-face."

"This wasn't what you expected?"

"No—and I feel certain I was right."

"What did you expect to find?"

Selby said, "That hole dug in the shack hadn't been there very long."

"You don't think Ezra Grolley dug it?"

"No."

"What makes you think that?"

"The pieces of sack that were in the hole weren't moldy. They would have been if they'd disintegrated in the damp ground. The sack wasn't dark in color, but was very much faded. . . . In short, that sacking wasn't ground-rotted, but was sun-rotted."

"But wasn't it damp?"

"Yes, it had been moistened before it was packed around the edges of the hole."

"Didn't Lossten do that?"

"Yes, I think he did so that he could have an authentic background for the will—after he'd found the hole. He went out to the cabin to find some place to plant the will. He found someone had been digging there, and when he found this hole he took advantage of the situation to put in the sacks and plant the will. I baited this trap because I wanted to catch the man who really dug the hole."

"Who was it, Doug," Sylvia asked, "A.B.C.?"

Selby shook his head. "Carr wouldn't touch a shovel for a thousand bucks."

"Who then?"

"Otto Larkin was in my office fumbling for cigarettes," Selby said. "I noticed that he had a blister on his right hand."

"Doug!" she exclaimed. "Do you think—"

He nodded.

"Oh, Doug, if we could only catch him. Can't we go back to the platform?"

"No. Our flashlights will have tipped him off—and anyway, I'm getting an idea, something I've overlooked."

"But suppose it *was* Larkin. Suppose Lossten doesn't go to Inez Stapleton's office. Suppose Larkin is waiting around here somewhere and gets his hands on Lossten?"

Selby said, "I didn't think of that until after I'd let Lossten go, and then I suddenly realized, when it was too late, what it would mean. . . . I'd be washed up, then. . . . Come on, Sylvia, we're going directly to Inez Stapleton's office and make certain that Lossten is waiting there."

But Inez Stapleton's office was dark and silent. There was no trace of Lossten. From a hotel lobby, Selby dialed the number of Inez's residence phone, and when he had her on the line, said, "This is Doug, Inez. What has happened to Lossten?"

"I told you, Doug, I don't know."

"Didn't he telephone you a little while ago and ask you to come to your office?"

"Why, no. I haven't heard from him."

"Or from Mrs. Lossten?"

"No. Why, Doug, what's happened?"

"Nothing," Selby said. "I was just checking up. If you do hear from him, please get in touch with me."

He hung up the telephone and turned to face Sylvia Martin's look of dismay.

"What's happened, Doug? Where is he?"

Selby said, "On a guess, Otto Larkin has him."

He turned abruptly away from her and walked over to stand in front of the window in the lobby of the hotel. Suddenly he turned. "I guess," he said slowly, "I should have realized earlier that the laws of evidence represent the conclusions gleaned from centuries of human experience. . . . When evidence is such that the law says it can't be used against a person, it's really because years of human experience have shown that it isn't to be depended on."

"What do you mean?"

His laugh was nervous and slightly apologetic. "I mean," he said, "that I've been so busy trying to find some way of getting around the laws of evidence in order to get a letter introduced in court that I haven't stopped to think— Come on, Sylvia, we're going places. Let's have a talk with our bank clerk, Elmer Stoker."

17

ELMER ANSWERED THE DOORBELL, SWITCHED ON THE porch light, and peered out. Then he opened the front door, and as he recognized them said nervously, and with a little too effusive cordiality, "Why, hello, Mr. Selby. How do you do, Miss Martin? Won't you folks come in? The family have gone to the movies. Are you getting anywhere with the murder?"

"I think so," Selby said, and then waited until they were seated in the living room before saying anything else. Then he looked Stoker over very deliberately. "You're feeling better than the last time I saw you," he decided.

Elmer Stoker fidgeted uncomfortably, started to say something, checked himself, and shifted his eyes.

"Elmer," Selby said, staring steadily at the young man, "you were pretty much broken up when you discovered that murder, weren't you?"

"I'll say I was. I hated to seem to be such a sissy, but it was the first time I'd ever seen anything like that. I suppose it's an old story to you, but it hit me right where I live. I couldn't have stayed in that room another minute—"

Selby interrupted his voluble explanation. "Elmer," he said, "you knew her, didn't you?"

Color drained from the young man's face. His lips quivered.

"You'd better tell me the truth," Selby said.

Elmer Stoker met his eyes. "Yes, I knew her."

"How long had you known her?"

"I met here about three months ago, right after she went back to work—after the baby was born."

"Tell me about it, Elmer."

"There isn't much to tell. I—I fell for her awfully hard. I— All right, I was in love with her."

"Go on. Tell us the rest of it."

"I was engaged to a girl at the time and— Well, that's all there is to it, Mr. Selby. I met Alice and within two weeks I was desperately in love."

"She was older than you?"

"I know it, but there wasn't a great difference in our ages. She was so wholesome and such a square shooter, I— Well, I just fell for her, that's all."

"And how about this girl to whom you were engaged?"

"Margaret. She— Well, I'd rather not talk about that, Mr. Selby. I'd been something of a fool and she was determined I was going to marry her and— Well, it was just a mess, that's all."

"What did you finally do about it?"

"I told the bank I wanted a transfer. They knew my folks lived in Madison City and thought that was where I wanted to go. So they transferred me here. Alice told me that she couldn't marry me. She wasn't even divorced, although she and her husband had separated. She told me to wait for six months and then we could see how we both felt. I think she cared for me a lot but— Well, that's the way it was."

"And you knew she was coming to Madison City?"

"No, I swear that I didn't."

"Didn't you arrange to meet her there in that house?"

"Honestly, I didn't. When I went in to that bedroom and saw the body on the floor and the condition of the room, I knew a murder had been committed and that I must telephone the sheriff. I put through the call right away and then went back. I don't think it was morbid curiosity, but I just couldn't keep my eyes off of it. . . . And then I recognized her."

"Why didn't you tell us at the time?"

"If I'd had another ten minutes before the under-sheriff came, I would have. But I was in a panic. I was afraid—afraid I was going to be mixed up in it, and I was sick, absolutely physically sick. I couldn't think. I could hardly talk."

"You were working in the bank in Oakland when you first met her?"

"Yes, sir."

"Who was this girl to whom you were engaged?"

"Can't we just leave her out of it, Mr. Selby? I'd hate to drag her in—"

"No. You've concealed too much already. Who was she?"

"Margaret Edwards."

"She lives in Oakland?"

"No. San Francisco."

"You've been corresponding with her recently?"

"Yes—of course."

"Seen her lately?"

"No."

"Where is she now?"

"In San Francisco. The Hillcrest Apartments."

"And you wrote to Alice Grolley?"

"Once or twice, yes. Just little notes. Not even anything personal in them. I felt she'd like it that way. I—I didn't know *what* to do, Mr. Selby."

The young man's lips quivered.

Abruptly, Selby pushed back his chair and got to his feet. "I want to use your phone," he said.

Selby dialed Sheriff Brandon's number, and when the sheriff answered, said, "Rex, I think we're headed for a show-down on that murder case. I want you to hide that Grolley baby where no one can see her. Put her in a safe place somewhere outside the house. . . . Haven't you a room up over the garage? . . . Well, let Mrs. Brandon take her up there, keep the door locked, and keep the child quiet. Don't have any lights on in the room. No one must know she's there. Absolutely no one."

It took Brandon a moment to adjust himself to the situation, then he said, "Okay, Doug. I'll do it right away."

Selby said, "I'll be out there in about ten minutes. Get the baby put away, then sit tight until I get there."

When Brandon had hung up, Selby dialed the number of A. B. Carr's residence.

Carr answered the plone almost immediately.

"Selby talking, Carr," the district attorney said, close-clipping his words as though he were under the stress of great excitement. "An attempt's been made to murder the Grolley baby. . . . No, I don't know the details. The child is hovering between life and death. Sheriff Brandon frightened the assailant. . . . There's going to be a lot of public feeling about this. I'm making a quick roundup. I'm asking you to find out where Teel is—or was twenty minutes ago, and let me know. You can call me at Brandon's house."

"I don't need to call you there," Carr said. "Teel is right here and has been here for the last hour."

"Where's your other client, Mrs. Hunter?"

"What does she have to do with it?"

"I'm just making a check-up, that's all."

"I'll have to find out and let you know," Carr said after a moment's silence.

"Do that, if you will, please," Selby said.

"But why should anyone want to murder that baby?"

"Why did anyone want to murder her mother?"

"But— But killing the baby wouldn't do any good," Carr said. "Even if the baby were killed, the property wouldn't revert to the Grolley estate."

"Suppose the mother left no heirs?"

"In that event, it's the Losstens you want to check up on. And Mrs. Grolley left a will, you know."

"I'm trying to check up on the Losstens."

"Take my tip," Carr said, "and do a *lot* of checking."

"I will," Selby said, and hung up.

Selby returned to the living room. "I want you to stay right here," he said to Elmer Stoker. "I'll call you later. Don't go to bed. Wait up for my telephone call."

He nodded to Sylvia Martin. "Let's go, Sylvia."

The night had turned muggy. The clouds seemed to have settled heavily until they hung over the city, piling up against the mountains, making the air close and, for a blessed relief, moist.

Selby made time out to the sheriff's house, whipped his car around into the driveway, slammed on the emergency brake, and was out through the door almost before the car had come to a dead stop. Brandon was waiting for him at the door of the vine-covered porch.

"What's the trouble, Doug?"

Selby said, "Let's get some lights on, quick, Rex. Where are your switches? I want the whole house ablaze with light. . . . Did Mrs. Brandon get the baby out of the way?"

The sheriff nodded toward a square garage building over which some previous tenant had built a servant's room. "She's up there," he said. "Made quite a stir about it, too, son; said that if we couldn't solve cases without snatching a baby out of a warm bed and sound sleep, we'd better take some lessons from Otto Larkin. . . . I told her that it was part of a game to disqualify Teel as guardian, and that made it all right."

"Getting to be some diplomat, aren't you?" Selby asked with a grin.

"Nope," Brandon disclaimed promptly. "Just a married man. You get that way after twenty or thirty years."

They went around the house, finding light switches and clicking them on. Sylvia Martin moved swiftly about the lower floor. Brandon and the district attorney climbed stairs to the upper floor. "Got time to tell me what it's all about?" Brandon asked as they started downstairs.

"I baited a trap," Selby said. "Lossten walked into it. I turned him loose when he promised to meet me at Inez Stapleton's office, and I'm afraid Larkin picked him up before he got there. You can figure what *that* will mean."

Brandon started to make some quick comment, but caught himself and waited for the space of two deep breaths. Then he said quietly, "Why did you do that, son?"

"What?"

"Turn him loose after you once had him."

"Because I thought he'd go to Inez Stapleton's office."

"It was taking a chance."

"It was," Selby admitted, "and I lost. I'd like to get

some other cars around here, Rex. Better call your office and have Bob Terry rush a couple of deputies out. I want people moving around the house—a lot of activity—keep the shades up and walk back and forth past the windows. Keep moving around from room to room, talking."

"Anything else?" Brandon asked.

"No. That's enough."

"Suppose you tell me what sort of a trap you're baiting this time."

Selby said, "I may not have time, Rex, but here's the dope. You can figure it for yourself. That alibi of Teel's is altogether too pat to have been accidental. It was carefully thought up for him by someone else who knew just what he was doing. That someone else was Old A.B.C. Of all the alibis in the world, Teel has one of the best."

"You mean he did it deliberately?" the sheriff asked.

"I think he must have. That means only one thing. He knew exactly when he'd want that alibi—in other words, within what time limits. Now here's another thing. Remember that Mrs. Grolley left no fingerprints there in the Glencannon ranch house, yet her gloves were found in the glove compartment of the Lossten automobile. The Lossten automobile was identified as the one which pushed that Hunter car off the grade.

. . . Yet here's something which doesn't jibe, Rex. Margaret Faye told one of the most dramatic moving stories on the witness stand I have ever heard. You'll remember her testimony at the coroner's inquest. . . . But her face never changed expression, not by so much as the flicker of an eyelash. She's not what you'd call an imaginative type. She's practical, selfish, poised— Rex, I'm sorry, but seconds are too precious. I just haven't the time to explain. You get the men up here fast. Keep them moving back and forth as I instructed, and carry on until you hear me call. I hate to ask you to play it blind, Rex, but—"

"Shucks, son, forget it," Brandon said, picking up the telephone and calling his office.

Selby shot out the back door and disappeared into the darkness.

18

THE FIRST LIGHT DROPS OF RAIN STARTED TO FALL AS
Selby waited, crouched in the shadows, some fifty feet
from the back of the garage in the rear of Sheriff
Brandon's house. Those first drops were hardly more
than a fine mist which could be felt only when a breath
of wind blew them against the skin. Gradually they became larger until they could be heard sifting against the
leaves and the shingles of the garage roof.

It was a big, rambling old-fashioned house and light
was pouring from every window. Figures walked back
and forth across those lighted windows, engaging in
mysterious conversation, furnishing an air of sinister
midnight activity.

Selby could feel the dampness sogging his clothes.
Consulting the luminous dial of his wrist watch, he felt
a strange uneasiness, as though something which must
happen according to the rules of logic had simply re-

fused to take place. It was as though a trusted adding machine suddenly persisted in giving a series of wrong answers to a simple problem of addition.

Then when he was on the point of yielding to his doubts, he heard a rustle in the darkness. A moment later, the blotch of a dark figure passed between him and the patch of illumination cast on the back yard by the light which poured out of one of the windows.

This figure slid stealthily into a pathway of shadow between the illumination emanating from two adjacent windows, walked quickly toward the house, avoiding the light.

Selby slipped from his place of concealment, tiptoed quietly along behind the figure bundled up in a coat, the collar turned up around the neck.

Selby stepped forward from the shadows. "Perhaps I could tell you what you want to know, Mrs. Hunter."

She gave a half scream, and for a moment seemed poised for quick flight, then resistance seemed to ooze from her and she burst into hysterical tears. "Tell me, tell me," she sobbed.

"About your child?"

"Yes, yes. What about her?"

Selby said, "You've done a very dangerous thing, Mrs. Hunter, a daring thing. You've . . ."

"But what about my baby? Never mind what *I've*

done. I can't stand this any longer. I've been going through hell. Where's my baby girl? Tell me, is *she* safe?"

"Yes. Would you like to see her?"

"Oh, yes! Yes, please!"

Selby took her by the arm. "We'll go inside," he said.

Sheriff Brandon stared at them with surprised eyes as they stood in the doorway, blinking in the illumination of the room, Mrs. Hunter's face drawn and strained, Selby gravely triumphant, his coat beaded with moisture, his hand holding Mrs. Hunter's trembling arm.

"Suppose you tell us about it," he said.

"I'll tell you anything—everything, but I've got to see my baby!"

"You can see her anyway, Mrs. Hunter, in just a few minutes, but it will be better if you tell us a few things first."

The words poured out in a flood. "I'm from San Francisco. I was employed by Mrs. Grolley as nursemaid for her little girl. I had a baby of my own of about the same age. That made it cheaper for her, because I needed some work I could do and still be with my child. When she and Teel planned the trip to Madison City they told me I was to come with them, but I said I'd have to bring my baby along. My God, I've been going crazy! When can I see her?"

"Tell us a little more," Selby urged gently.

"Well, we started for Madison City. Mr. Teel decided to take a short cut through from the San Francisco highway. It didn't say it was a bad mountain road. I was riding with Mrs. Grolley in her car. Her baby was in the rear. My baby was back with Teel in his car."

"Why wasn't your baby in the car with you?" Selby asked.

"During the afternoon I'd been riding with Mr. Teel, and my baby was with me. Then when it got dark, Mrs. Grolley was a little afraid to be driving alone, and I went up with her. My baby was asleep so I left her in the car with Teel."

"Go on," Selby said. "What happened?"

"We were driving down that mountain grade. It was a bad road, and Mrs. Grolley wasn't too good on mountain roads. And she wouldn't turn off the lights in the car."

"And Teel was behind you?"

"Yes."

"All of a sudden a car came up from behind, driving fast. A woman was driving it—"

"Margaret Faye?" Selby interrupted.

"Yes. How did you know?"

"Never mind. Tell us just what happened."

"Well, I have never seen a woman so wrought up. I could just see her white face. It was all twisted with rage. She drove up fast on the inside and screamed some names at us. At first, I thought she was talking to me. Then I turned to Mrs. Grolley to say that the woman must be crazy, and as soon as I saw Mrs. Grolley's face I knew it was something else."

"And then?" Selby asked.

"And then," she said, "we were on a bad hairpin curve, and Mrs. Grolley was so excited she could hardly control the car, and I felt a jar on the inside fenders. That woman had hit us near the front wheel. She did it deliberately. Well, you know what happened after that. Mrs. Grolley completely lost control of the car. I was thrown into the clear. She wasn't."

"And after that?"

"I was unconscious. The next thing I knew I was in Teel's car and he was driving toward Madison City, and when he saw I was conscious, he started talking to me. He told me that there had been a terrible accident, that Mrs. Grolley and her baby had both been killed, that he'd been close enough to see the whole thing, that he'd speeded up and overtaken the other car, that the woman was jealous of Mrs. Grolley, and had deliberately driven her off the road."

"And then he suggested that if you'd keep quiet and let him substitute babies for the time being he'd make it worth your while?"

"Not then, he didn't. That came later after we got into town and he stopped to telephone."

"He telephoned Carr—his lawyer?"

"I don't know to whom he telephoned. All I know is he put through the call. He was talking on the telephone for quite a while. Then he came back and told me what to do."

"What was that?"

"I was to go to San Francisco and get the license plates off my car so that he could put them on Mrs. Grolley's car. And my baby was to be substituted for the Grolley baby. I didn't want to, of course, but he pointed out to me how much it would mean to me, and how my baby could have everything in the world that it needed."

"Did you know anything about Grolley's sister?"

"Teel told me something. He said he was going to have to drag her into it in order to keep her on the defensive. That was the way he put it. He said something about borrowing her car to rig the stage."

"How did he know all about her, and where her automobile could be located?"

"He'd had a detective agency shadowing her for ten days," Mrs. Hunter said. "A man had followed them all the way out from Louisiana. I found that out afterwards."

"And when did you find out that Margaret Faye was the one who had been driving that other car?"

"Just before the inquest. They told me that I wasn't to let on that I recognized her. . . . By that time, I was into it so deep that I had to see it through."

"You went to San Francisco the day after the accident?"

"Yes. They sent me up to get the license plates."

"And Carr told Margaret Faye what to say?"

"I guess so. I don't know."

"Then they planted Mrs. Grolley's body in the ranch house?"

"Yes. I think they used Mrs. Lossten's car for that. They wanted to drag her into it."

"Did you meet Mr. Carr at all?"

"Yes. I took a ride with him out to Mr. Grolley's house the morning after the accident."

"Did he go in?"

"Yes."

"Did you?"

"No."

"Did you have any conversation with Mr. Carr about what you were to do?"

"Not with him. Mr. Teel told me that I wasn't to talk to him about what was happening—just to go with him. . . . I think that if anyone had seen Mr. Carr going into the house, I was supposed to be Mrs. Grolley; but no one told me that definitely."

"Then you weren't in the bus station except long enough to leave your baby there?"

"That's right. And then I was driven out to the Glencannon house, and Mr. Teel had some new clothes for me, and I took my clothes off and gave them to Mr. Teel, and he went into the bedroom and put them on Mrs. Grolley's body. There was some woman in there. I don't know who it was. I think it was Margaret Faye, but I can't swear to that. I *think* Mr. Teel caught up with her there on the grade, and told her she was going to be convicted of murder unless she co-operated with him. . . ."

"I don't understand," Brandon broke in.

Selby turned to him swiftly. "You will," he promised. "Just one more thing, Mrs. Hunter. It *was* you who telephoned me pretending to be Mrs. Grolley?"

She nodded miserably.

The doorbell rang. Brandon looked inquisitively at Selby.

"Sure," the district attorney said, "let's see who it is. . . . Have you sent someone out to ask Mrs. Brandon to bring the baby in?"

"Yes."

Brandon opened the door. Carr stood on the threshold. It was raining now, a gentle, persistent drizzle, and water had collected on the brim of the lawyer's hat, glistened on the surface of his raincoat where the lights fell on it.

The man's personality was as dominant as ever, his smile as magnetic. He was there to face crushing defeat, to try to salvage what he could by the sheer ingenuity of his cunning mind, yet his manner held all of its customary poise. Neither cringing nor yet defiant, he stood outlined against the pattering rain which drifted down just beyond the roof of the porch.

"Good evening," he said, "—or perhaps I should say good morning. I just dropped in to see— Ah, *there* you are, my dear!"

Mrs. Hunter said simply, "I *had* to come."

"Yes," Carr said, "I shouldn't have told you. I realized that you would have to come—when I stopped to think." His needle-sharp eyes looked over Selby's face, glanced at Brandon, and then returned to Mrs. Hunter. "What have you told them?" he asked.

"The truth," she said.

Selby said, "Rather clever, Carr. It was quick think-ing. If Mrs. Grolley and her child outlived Ezra Grol-ley, they came into a small fortune. If they died before him, the fortune went to the sister."

"Very interesting," Carr said, smiling. "I suppose you know I can't admit to having the slightest idea of what you're talking about."

"And so," Selby went on, "you decided to convince everyone that Mrs. Grolley died *after* her husband. You borrowed the Lossten automobile, first to involve them in the case and also to take the body to the Glen-cannon bungalow out of the way until you were ready to set the stage. . . . Ezra Grolley was dying, so you knew you wouldn't have long to wait."

Carr said, "My *dear* young man, I'm quite certain that no matter how willing Mrs. Hunter may have been to curry your official favor, she never told you any such thing. You're drawing on your imagination. . . . And if Mrs. Hunter *did* tell you anything of the sort, she's distraught, nervous and not in a mentally responsible condition. Isn't that right, my dear?"

She shook her head. "I'm not going through with it, Mr. Carr. I can't. My daughter won't have any money, but she'll have something else, a clean slate. Teel got me into this and kept pushing me along, but I've been thinking. I'm not going along any further."

Carr made clicking noises with his tongue against the roof of his mouth. "You should see a doctor. You must be in a very serious state."

Selby said, "I'm afraid this time, Carr, you've got yourself in a mess out of which you can't wriggle. There's too much corroborative evidence."

Carr raised his finely-shaped brows. "*I've* got *myself* in a mess? Good Heavens, Selby, don't tell me this hysteria is contagious. I've always had a high regard for your intelligence. Don't spoil it now. I don't know what this woman has told you, but, putting two and two together, it would seem that Mr. Teel, my client, may perhaps have carried an innocent deception a little too far. Even so, you'll have a hard time finding any definite crime on which to convict him. . . . As for myself—come, come, let's be reasonable. Regardless of what my *client* may or may not have done, I can assure you that *I* knew absolutely nothing about it. I believe this young woman will tell you frankly that she never had any contact with me in any way except that she retained me to file suit against Mrs. Lossten."

"I rode out to Grolley's house with you Thursday morning," Mrs. Hunter protested.

"And a delightful outing it was," Carr agreed smilingly.

"Was it later you changed your clothes and gave

them to Teel to put on Mrs. Grolley's body?" Selby demanded.

"Did he really do that?" Carr asked, as though the information was new to him and aroused both curiosity and interest, but no apprehension in his mind.

"You know you told Teel what to have me do," Mrs. Hunter burst out.

Carr shook his head sadly, "Such a foolish notion! Mr. Teel will tell you how utterly wrong you are."

"And you told him to tell me to sue Mrs. Lossten."

"My *dear* young woman," Carr said, his voice holding a note of horrified incredulity, "do you mean to tell me that you thought *I* suggested you file a false suit? I'm amazed." He shook his head sadly. "I am afraid that there is more to this than I had thought. I was on the point of telling you, Mr. Selby, that I was about to withdraw from representing Teel. . . . But now that my name has been dragged into the matter, in justice to myself I will have to vindicate Mr. Teel.

"I can assure you that while Teel may have been betrayed by an impulsive generosity and a natural love for an attractive child—you remember I told you something of his charities—he has been guilty of no crime—absolutely no crime, Counselor. . . . Search your penal code, and you'll find I'm right."

Selby said grimly, "We'll look into that."

Carr said, "You must admit that when the circumstances are skillfully presented, a jury will sympathize with the man and with this young mother."

"That," Selby admitted, "is the dangerous part of it."

Carr's grin was sardonic. "And I can assure you that Teel's case will be skillfully presented. . . . You can count on that, Selby."

"It had better be, because I am going to prosecute Margaret Edwards, who has described herself as Margaret Faye, a hitchhiking waitress, for first-degree murder. I'm going to prosecute Teel for compounding a felony. I am going to give Mrs. Hunter immunity for turning state's evidence."

Carr shrugged his shoulders. "You might convict Miss Faye of manslaughter due to criminal negligence in driving her car," he said. "You might convict Teel of compounding a felony.—I'm sure I can't say. Juries are so sympathetic and so uncertain, but you'll never get a first-degree murder conviction."

"I may not try," Selby said. "I may only try for second-degree or first-degree without the death penalty."

Carr was thoughtful. "My clients," he said, "might offer to plead guilty if you didn't try to convict them of crimes which they didn't commit."

"You'd have them plead guilty so that *you* can save *your* bacon?" Selby asked.

Carr once more clicked his tongue against the roof of his mouth. "You are *so* prone to jump at conclusions, Counselor."

"One of these days you're going to burn your own fingers—*good*," Rex Brandon blurted out.

Taking a cigar from his pocket, Carr carefully clipped off the end, struck a match, and held it to the tip of the cigar. Then he watched the match burn down almost to his fingers, but just before it reached his hand, he suddenly blew it out and dropped the charred stick into an ash tray.

When he had done that, he looked at Sheriff Brandon significantly—and laughed.

19

RAIN WAS FALLING STEADILY, A GENTLE, SOAKING RAIN which disappeared almost immediately into the thirsty ground. A southeast wind was freshening steadily.

Selby and Sylvia Martin drove toward the city jail, the windshield wiper of Selby's car clicking monotonously back and forth, clearing a semicircular path of visibility.

"How did you know, Doug?" Sylvia Martin asked, and it was hard for her to keep the triumph from her voice.

He laughed. "I didn't *know!* I did a lot of suspecting. The fact that Teel had such a pat alibi, the fact that Mrs. Grolley had left no fingerprints— Oh, there were a dozen things that just didn't click. . . . Margaret Faye told a moving, dramatic story of what had happened and how it had happened. You could just see it unfolding in front of your eyes. It was a story which held everyone in the room breathless. Yet she wasn't the type who would ordinarily tell a story that way. She'd have said, 'We were driving along in the automobile. Mrs. Grolley lost control. I was thrown out, and the car must have rolled on down the canyon with the baby in it.'

"Of course *that* story wouldn't have been so convincing. So Carr wrote out what she was to say to make a convincing story. But they slipped up in not having her put some expression into her face. A woman who had sufficient delicacy of perception to have seen and remembered all of those dramatic details would have been dramatic herself."

"But if Carr told her exactly what to say, coached her, and—"

"He didn't," Selby said. "If Carr had ever seen her in dress rehearsal, he'd have fixed all that. But Carr was keeping in the background. He wrote out the story and gave it to Teel. Teel was the one who drilled her. . . . Carr was too smart to trust these women. Only Teel had a point of contact with him."

"What else did you have for a clue?" she asked.

"Lots of things, the blood drops particularly. Did you notice the way those blood drops had little spatters all around the edges?"

"Why, yes. You showed me that."

"Showed you that they were dropped from about the height of a person's head. They were dropped at regular intervals, but those spatters were evenly distributed. If they'd come from Mrs. Grolley, and she had been engaged in a struggle, they wouldn't have been like that. When blood drops from a person who is moving, even at a walk, the liquid is thick enough so that there's a carry-forward momentum which disrupts the drop as it falls, and makes a secondary drop in the direction of the motion.

"My own investigation showed me that, but I took occasion to check up afterwards. In Gross's book on criminal investigation, there's a complete discourse on the subject, with diagrams showing just how drops of blood behave under the circumstances. . . . And another thing. Notice that when we found Mrs. Grolley's baggage at the bus station with the baby, we found typewritten directions for the feeding and care of the infant. . . . No mother would have had that so conveniently located unless she had expected there was a possibility the infant would fall into the hands of strangers. She might have had some notes or perhaps some feeding formula given her by a physician, but a complete typewritten list of directions— No, it all pointed to the same thing, when I once began to suspect what that thing was.

"I became suspicious when I went to San Francisco—not that I then suspected *exactly* what had happened—but I appreciated the possibilities, without having my suspicions definitely crystallize. But I took fingerprints from the toys in Mrs. Grolley's apartment. . . . Carr, of course, had anticipated this. He'd seen to it that the toys belonging to the Hunter baby had been planted there.

"Later on, when I began to check up on things, I realized those toys were too prominently displayed. A mother would have taken most of those toys with her. . . . Then I remembered that the witness who had seen the woman who left the baby at the stage depot—Mrs. Albert Purdy, the one who was going to Albuquerque—had said the woman was a *blonde*, dressed in light tan clothes. Mrs. Grolley was a brunette, but because the clothes matched so exactly, I didn't at first realize the significance of the discrepancy.

"When I was in San Francisco, I found a letter Mrs. Grolley had been writing, apparently to some woman, mentioning the fact that she was going to Madison City, that she would, of course, see 'E.' while she was there. I assumed, of course, that she was referring to Ezra and that the letter was to Mrs. Lossten, particularly because she mentioned a difference in ages, and that the letters she had from E. had been very stilted, conventional letters. . . . That just shows how easy it is to walk into a trap when you start investigating evidence with a preconceived notion. The fact that she mentioned in that letter that she had to go on other business not connected with the person referred to as 'E.' should have tipped me off that I was on the wrong track; but it didn't. . . . I shudder to think of what would have happened if I'd kept working on that theory —gone into court and tried to convict Mrs. Lossten of the murder. If I could have introduced that letter in evidence, it would have been almost conclusive so far as a jury was concerned—and an innocent woman would have been convicted."

They reached the city jail, and rushed up the cement walk, their heads down, pushing against the beat of a rain which had now become a downpour.

Selby rang the night bell and was admitted by the turnkey. Otto Larkin was at the telephone. An expression of self-satisfaction suffused his face. "Oh, hello, Selby," he said, and then said into the telephone, "Wait just a minute." He put his hand over the mouthpiece. "You kinda slipped up tonight, didn't you?" he asked, and the gloating triumph of his voice showed that he no longer felt it necessary to retain the mask of official hypocrisy.

Sylvia Martin couldn't resist breaking it to him. "If

that fatuous smile of yours is because you're just engaged in telephoning the *Blade* about how smart *you* are, and how Doug Selby let a prisoner slip through his fingers, you can hang up and forget about it." She looked at him gloatingly. "We just dropped in to tell you the murder of Mrs. Grolley is solved."

The chief observed the calm confidence of her eyes and manner, and his own expression of self-satisfaction faded. The receiver left his ear almost mechanically. He replaced it on the hook, pushed the telephone from him.

"Huh!" he said.

Inez Stapleton came in just as Selby finished outlining the recent developments to the crestfallen chief. She went at once to Selby.

"Doug, I just heard what happened. Sheriff Brandon called me up."

"Well, congratulations," Selby drawled. "Despite the fact your clients tried to steal the estate through a forged will, they get it anyway."

Inez said, "They only get half of it, Doug. Carr slipped over a fast one. Just this afternoon he called on me. He suggested that we should quit our fighting, that the estate would all be wasted in attorneys' fees, and that it would be better to split the thing fifty-fifty. He had an agreement all drawn up providing that, regardless of who was legally entitled to the estate, we would divide it fifty-fifty, Mrs. Lossten getting half, and the child the other half."

"Did he describe the child as the Grolley baby?" Selby asked.

Inez flushed. "No, he didn't. I thought there was something queer about it at the time, but it just didn't register, Doug. That man's a skunk."

"How *did* he describe her?"

"As the baby for the care, custody, and guardianship of which one Jackson Teel had filed application for letters of guardianship, as the daughter of Ezra Grolley, said baby being now in the physical custody of Mrs. Rex Brandon."

Selby grinned.

"And," she went on angrily, "there was a clause in that agreement that each side was making the agreement with full knowledge of all of the circumstances, with the advice of competent legal counsel, and that there would never afterwards be any claim of fraud, duress, or undue influence."

"Did your clients sign it?"

"Apparently they did. I gave Carr a letter that the agreement met with my approval, if it suited my clients —and gave him permission to submit it to them. I didn't know where they were. Really I didn't, Doug.

They were in hiding somewhere. But Old A.B.C. must have tailed them. He called me two hours later to tell me the agreement had been signed."

"But Doug caught Lossten digging out in the Grolley orchard," Sylvia Martin said. "Why would he have done that—if the agreement had been signed?"

Selby shrugged. "Anything he found simply wouldn't have appeared in the inventory as a part of the estate. . . . He'd have kept it all."

Inez Stapleton nodded. "He might even have kept it from his wife. . . . That was a filthy trick of Carr's, slipping that settlement over on us. I'm going to go to court over it."

Selby laughed. "You'll have a sweet time. When you try to allege fraud, Carr will bring up that forged will. Your clients can't ask the aid of a court of equity in setting that agreement aside unless they can come into court with clean hands. Don't forget that forged will! And Lossten going up to San Francisco to plant that forged letter in the jewel case! How did he get into that apartment? He must be as clever with a jimmy as a pen. You certainly do have nice people for clients. No, the pot is just about as black as the kettle, Inez."

"I didn't know, Doug. I felt simply terrible when I found out about those forgeries. I—I told them I wasn't going to represent them any more, and then Carr showed up with this agreement suggesting we settle it all."

"The old fox," Selby said. He turned to Larkin. "Well, tomorrow's going to be a big day, Chief, so I'll wish *you* good night."

Inez Stapleton said, "Well, *I'm* not going to wish him good night. I came down here for the specific purpose of getting Terry B. Lossten released from custody. You had absolutely no right to arrest him for that murder, Otto Larkin, and I guess you know it by this time."

"Well," Larkin said, in a blustering attempt to defend his position, "there was circumstantial evidence that—"

"Birdseed!"

Larkin, red in the face, said to the turnkey, "Bring out Terry Lossten."

"But let *me* out before you do," Selby said. "I have my beauty sleep to consider."

"And *I* have a story to write," Sylvia Martin announced.

As the turnkey opened the jail door, Inez Stapleton put her hand on Doug's arm. "Thanks, Doug. You're—you're grand!"

The turnkey flung the door wide open. Sylvia Martin and Doug Selby looked out at the drenching downpour which was cascading from the heavens, then at each other.

Suddenly Selby chuckled and turned back to Inez.

"What's funny?" she demanded.

"Inez, whose goose was that you were talking to me about the other day up at the office?"

"I'm glad, Doug," she said simply.

Sylvia said, "All right, Doug, we make a run for it."

Doug pulled his hat down low on his forehead. "Ready. *Go!*"

They sprinted down the walk toward the car. Behind them, Inez Stapleton watched wistfully—then the jail door clanged sullenly shut.

THE END